the write before christmas

EVERGREEN LAKE: UNDER THE MISTLETOE

LYNESSA LAYNE

For Julie
RIP

CHRISTMAS TRAIN

WINTER TREE FARM

ICE SKATING RINK

LIPS & HIPS

EVERGREEN ROAD

SIPS ON MAIN

READ BETWEEN
THE WINES

TOWN
SQUARE

GINGERBREADS

MAIN STREET

NADINE'S
NURSERY

POLICE STATION

CHAMBER OF
COMMERCE

HANSON'S
MERCANTILE

FAIR ROAD

FIRE DEPT.

LIBRARY

MECHANIC

CHURCH

WELCOME TO
Evergreen
LAKE

SKI LODGE
THIS WAY

FOR SALE

EVERGREEN LAKE INN

LAKE STREET

SANTA'S
CLOSET

EVERGREEN
PET RESCUE

POWDER
ROOM

THE REINDEER HOLE

LAKE SHORE DRIVE

EVERGREEN
LAKE

CHRISTMAS
FESTIVAL

one

KAMRIE

I ADJUSTED my lanyard and crossed my legs, stared up at the stage from the front row. Though I appeared impassive, my belly fluttered every time the man being interviewed looked over the audience.

Was he making eye contact or was I imagining things?

The interviewer, a famous news anchor turned fiction author, laughed at some witty comment I missed. The audience chuckled with her, so I did, too. Her subject, lounging in his plush chair opposite, grinned at me like he saw right through my inattentive response.

He could be looking beyond me, right?

Depending on the lighting in their faces, they probably couldn't see anyone and were pretending, something both onstage did well.

"Tom," the news anchor called his attention to her face again. "Tell us the truth, you created the Detective Grayer series with the plan of playing him in the TV series, didn't you?"

Again, the audience laughed with Tom's charming chuckle. His hair fell over his eye and he flipped the salted pepper to the

1

side. "I wish. If I'd known going in, I would've started working out from the time I was ten." Another audience laugh.

"You trained with the military to earn your role as Detective Grayer, isn't that correct?"

Tom nodded. "I did. He's a hardened veteran, forcibly retired from the special operations community. There's a very specific vibe I wrote for him. In that regard, he takes after my uncle. It's my way to honor his service and bring to light the resentment of a warrior put on the shelf in the prime of his life. My uncle carries this constant regret like survivors' guilt. He admitted he never planned to make it to retirement."

"Did you not like the actor chosen for the role?"

Tom scoffed. "I loved him in that movie he was in three years ago. I asked for him specifically, but I think the director grew tired of my interruptions during filming. He was halfway through the pilot when he finally snapped and told me if I could do it better, then I needed to audition like the actor I'd chosen. What can I say?" Tom shrugged. "When I have a vision, I can't rest until I bring it to life exactly the way it looks in my mind."

"Was this your first audition?" she asked.

He arched a brow at her. Her grin broadened. She knew better. As did any Tom Snow fan.

Tom said, "My fans will likely know this, but to be fair—wait." He looked over the audience. "Raise your hand if you're new to my work."

I looked around. About one-third of the audience raised their hands. Tom sat back and sent the interviewer an apologetic grimace, then grinned at the newcomers. His eyes skimmed the front row. "Raise your hand if you're already a fan."

The interviewer clapped and laughed. "You're asking for trouble, Tom."

"I'm asking for honesty and I'll explain why in a second."

Most everyone else raised their hands. My palms remained folded on my lap, but my heart pounded as he read the room and took note of my un-raised hand. His famous character, Detective Grayer, was a cocky, arrogant, know-it-all who got too much correct and solved far too many cases to be believable. For an investigative journalist turned evening broadcast news anchor, turned streaming TV star, I felt his work was contrary to the truth we with press passes knew too well.

Tom thanked the audience. "No, it wasn't my first audition by a long shot. My mom used to do small stage productions when I was little and I was painfully shy. She let me paint and design the sets with her, then she nudged me toward auditioning with her for a mother/son pair needed for one of the plays. Once I realized I could be someone other than Br— excuse me, Tom, I fell in love with acting."

My brow twitched. *Was that a slip of the tongue or a stutter?* I couldn't recall a time Tom Snow hiccuped in his delivery, even live.

He continued. "Do you all remember that commercial with the kid jumping his bike, then at the end pumping his fist with a cast on his arm? Yeah." He pointed his thumbs at himself with a cheesy pride. "Mom and Dad let me and my twin brother do a few commercials. He lost interest, mine grew. My parents were against Hollywood, so they refused to let me take acting classes, but told me if I worked to earn them and paid the bill, they wouldn't stop me."

The interviewer sat forward with a serious concern overtaking her previous pep. "You say you never set out to be a journalist, that it happened by accident. Your legacy would prove you have a natural ability. That the calling found you." She sent a sympathetic smile. "It must've been hard for you to expose the director of the off-Broadway play you starred in."

Tom gave a nervous laugh with a smile that didn't meet his

eyes. "Yeah, we lost our show. For some of us, that was our first big break. Believe it or not, the hardest part, you know, after accepting the truth about someone you used to admire and idolize, was finding a camera small enough before these awesome spy stores existed."

"You improvised with nanny-cams, correct?" she asked.

"I did." Tom nodded.

"Tell us about that."

Poor Tom. But this was juicy stuff even twenty years later.

"We were just teens. Some of us weren't yet old enough to vote. I think I was about nineteen, so as one of the older cast members, I felt a strong conviction to lead and protect. My friend opened up about being abused," Tom said. "Then one friend turned to two. My parents always said with critical thinking, what's popular isn't always right and what's right isn't always popular. You have to pull yourself out of the opinion and when two or more sources say the same thing without consulting with or knowing each other, there's a there there. That make sense?"

The audience murmured agreements. I squirmed a little, feeling guilty for my previous thoughts on his detective novels turned popular TV.

Tom continued. "I hadn't experienced anything negative myself, but I couldn't just sit, so I bought the whole cast these teddy bears and told them and the director that it was something my acting coach taught me to help me get more into my characters." Tom gestured with his open palm toward the audience like we might step into his hand so he could pull us closer. "This was before emotional support animals and such. I fooled all of them into thinking that this was merely an exercise. That they were to carry their teddy bear everywhere they went, test reactions of their peers, endure the hardships of being made fun of so their emotions would play for the audience. To use the bear like a child does. Really sold some bullshit to kids who'd put down toys far sooner than most for the very adult world of acting and fame. Pardon my French."

We all coughed a collective nervous laugh like we needed the comic relief under the weight of his testimony.

He licked his dry lips and looked the interviewer in the eyes. "Caught him on four nanny-cams inside those bears. They'd brought the bears everywhere but the showers. I never watched the footage. I didn't want to. I trusted my friends and when I confessed to the cameras inside the bears, they had what they needed to put that creep in prison."

We all clapped. I stood with the hundreds around me.

Was this why Mom wanted me to come to this interview?

I swallowed my worry for her. She didn't have much time left. I shouldn't be here. I should be watching episodes of Detective Grayer with her and giving her meds, baths, snacks.

I booked this convention over a year ago. Life had other plans. Fortunately, I have a daughter who writes and can always use more growth. I promise not to die until after you get back and tell me if he's as handsome in person.

I fought a private smile at her words in my mind and returned to my seat.

Tom thanked the audience, spoke about how his first interview on the case was so well-done, he'd scored a job with a news station, how he'd climbed the hours from early morning to evening reports. His detective novels came as a break from the heaviness of the news.

"Do you miss it?" The interviewer crossed her legs at the ankle, rested her chin in her hand, elbow on the arm of the chair.

"Sometimes, but Grayer is so much fun to play, I find myself eager to get back to the computer to write more stories for him in my off-time. I love my job."

She cast an indulgent smile. "I'm sure it's painful having to kiss Detective Grayer's wife."

Tom waved her away while he laughed. "It's all very professional. Remember, they've filed for divorce. Grayer can't win at his job *and* at romance at the same time. Most cops have the same problem. Sure, he's heroic, but he's also flawed. Tunnel vision. Loses track of those around him when he's on the hunt. Recipe for a disastrous love life."

I made duck lips, then rubbed them together when he seemed to catch my skepticism.

"Novels or television? Which one does the audience prefer? Show of hands." Tom watched each group raise their hands at his questions, then nodded. "Writer?" Hands rose, including mine. "Reader?" Mine rose again while the audience participated. "Jean, this brings me back to why I was asking these questions, because at every conference I'm asked for the magic ingredients to successful writing, like if I sprinkle some in my palm and blow it out into the audience, talent will erupt into a host of new novels and television shows, films."

Tom stood from his chair and paced the stage. He pointed to the sky. "When I sit to write, God doesn't come down and use my fingers, neither do demons or some writing fairy."

I couldn't help myself. I clapped with only two others. After three days of panels and interviews on the subject of writing, I was tired of hearing different recipes and people saying they weren't part of it, like the process was a type of possession that overtook them. When I sat to write, I sat *to write* and did what I had to. No fluff. Just work. Did I cry at times? Yeah, then I wrote with tears on my fingers and wiped the keyboard later. Did I ruin lives in my job? Yes. Did I sleep at night? Yes. Because for every life ruined, I'd saved the world from being preyed upon by the criminal in disguise ever again. Granted, Tom Snow wrote fiction. I wrote exposés.

Tom pointed down at me. "Thank you. You've been unwilling to participate as much as the rest of the class." My mouth dropped. "Nope. No arguing. I see all from up here." He cast his charming smile at his audience, little wink, then paced again. "She's not a fan of mine, again, no use arguing." He stopped in the center of the stage and opened his hands. "It's precisely my point. When you raised your hands, not everyone did. If I entertain even a fraction of the room, then I've done my job. I don't have to be the most popular person in the room and I'm not writing for everyone. I'm writing for Detective Grayer's audience. Not walking on eggshells to please the masses."

I licked my lips. My sweaty palms gripped together until my knuckles turned white.

"Just write the damn book. Grow your craft with the wisdom of others at these conferences, but write. You can't publish or even edit what doesn't exist outside your brain." Tom Snow drew a dash with his fingertip, autographed the air in front of him, cited the year like a quote in a book.

He bowed, then made us all laugh when he curtsied with his hands out like he pinched a skirt at his sides, crossed ankles.

Tom's hands cupped in prayer at his chest. "Thank you for having me. It's been an honor to be here."

TOM SHOOK hands with the interviewer, then waved as we were dismissed to our next classes in the busy schedule. I sidestepped people gathering in cliques and couples. They shared their programs and pointed at panels they planned to attend.

I'd tired of too many bodies in one place, too many puffy heads, too little authentic advice pertaining to my type of craft. Hell, some panels were overtaken by moderators so eager to promote their own work they barely gave time to the panelists. What was the point? I'd gleaned a few golden nuggets I'd take with me, but I wasn't a novelist. Poor Mom. She'd always planned to write a memoir about her life as a legendary news-caster in a time when women were more popular as eye-candy than serious journalists. This conference was something she'd signed up for before her diagnosis. She'd sent me as her proxy so six-hundred dollars didn't go to waste, or so she'd claimed. We both knew meeting Tom Snow was what she was really after.

A good daughter would've joined the masses at the eleva-tors to go meet Tom and get his autograph on his newest novel.

I opted for the stairs and found good company with other intro-verts eager for personal space.

"He was more likable in person," the lady next me said to the man with her. "I figured his head might be too big to fit through the elevator doors."

He laughed while I grinned to myself and watched the steps we trotted down. "They don't use the common elevators like us peasants. They have pathways behind the walls to keep them safe from fanatics."

I turned to the next flight.

"Oh, so I should've said something about his head fitting between the walls?" she quipped.

"You *do* know characters are just that, right?" the man asked. "He's not Grayer. He said so himself, he doesn't condone some of his detective's methodology. Doesn't cheat on his part-ners. Doesn't alienate friends and family."

"Pft. I went to the panel he was on," she said. "I had to get there an hour early just to get a good seat. Someone asked if his parents are proud of him, if they ever come to his premier parties or if he's still close to his siblings."

"What did he say?"

We rounded the next corner and trotted down the final flight.

"He said he keeps his family out of his work world."

The man shrugged. "What's wrong with that?"

"I think it means he doesn't have contact with his family anymore. He's a cliché. Got too big for the small town he comes from, too big to return to his roots …"

I lost track of their conversation as they melted into the throngs on the ground floor rushing for the restaurants and panel rooms. I beelined for the path toward the hotel rooms of this insane resort like a city within a city, beneath its own glass ceiling. The one blessing of this madness was that Mom booked an accessible room for the walker she'd used when she could still walk without assistance.

Directly off the convention center floor, I went down a ramp leading to a hallway and tapped my keycard against the pad.

"Miss Kole."

I jumped and dread filled my stomach. I yanked my hotel room door closed and twirled to face the kind fan of my mother's. I'd made the mistake of sitting beside him at a panel yesterday. He was young. How was I to know he'd somehow know of Evelyn Krouse?

My keycard tucked into my back pocket with my hand. I summoned a kind smile, though I loathed this guy knew my room number now. "Is this your room?" He gestured to the door at my back. "Man, you got lucky."

"Um, no. Mine is on the other end of the resort."

"Mine feels half a mile away. I counted. 458 steps from my door to the convention floor."

He peered over my shoulder like I was being creepy at someone's door. I blurted, "I was just checking on my mom."

"Oh, is she in there? Can I meet her?"

Crap!

"No, sorry. She's not well, which is why she's not at any of the panels."

"I'm sorry to hear that. There's a rumor going around that you're going to speak to honor her career tomorrow. Is that true?"

Was this guy a journalist? I suddenly got major vibes of a slipping cover, but why would a journalist be sniffing for information on my mom when she'd retired years ago?

"The rumors are tentative, but true. If she's rough, I'll be taking her home instead."

"I'm sorry to hear she's sick." He looked down the hallway. I did, too; we were alone. Why did I get the creeps? He plastered a jovial smile like he sensed my unease. "I'm about to go to the *Who Says Crime Doesn't Pay* panel and wondered if you wanted to sit with me? It starts in about five minutes. Shia Slayer is a panelist. I know you said you liked her work."

Did I say that in the small time we'd sat near each other?

I swallowed. "No, thanks. I've met her, but that's very thoughtful of you. I've got to feed Mom. Family first."

He studied my face like he didn't believe me. "Priorities, yeah. Understandable. You going to the mystery readings tonight? They're giving away free books."

"Depends if my mom needs me. Always hard to tell with her illness. If it's a good night, I'll see you there."

"Is she contagious? Should the attendees be worried?"

"No," I rushed. "It's not that type of illness or we wouldn't jeopardize the public like that."

Nervousness castrated his calm. "Of course, I'm sorry. I didn't mean to—"

"It's okay."

He said he'd save me a seat at his table. "Or, in line if you end up early enough. I was told it fills up fast and it's limited to the first hundred people."

"Sure." I nodded and pretended my phone was ringing. The device met my ear. "Yeah. That was me, don't worry. I ran into a fan of yours in the hall. Don't worry, I told him of your condition." I sent him a reassuring smile he seemed pleased with. "Yeah. Oh, that reminds me, I need to stop by my room for that soup you wanted." I waved at him, mouthed *he have fun*, then turned to hustle further down the hall until I lost sight of him lingering in front of my room like he memorized the number. "Well, after you said you had a craving, I went and bought some. Uh, huh." I kept pretending just in case.

Poor fake Mom. How did she and others like Tom Snow, hell, even the anchor who'd interviewed him, manage their fame? I'd been asked to take photos with people who'd stop in their tracks like they saw an apparition of Mom thirty years younger. Before I'd made my own small reputation by changing my last name, I was always asked about being my mother's daughter, if I'd followed in her footsteps to carry her legacy, if I ever planned to be behind my own news desk one day. Sometimes, I lied and said I didn't know who people were talking about. Most of my generation didn't know her. Their parents always gave me away.

Once certain he'd vanished, I lazed back toward my true hotel room. My thumbs flew over the keypad on my phone, then I thought better of texting. A second later, Mom's tired voice filled my ear. Relief swept my prior stress under the rug. I'd see the mess when the time came to clean under there, but for now I could pretend all was spiffy and normal.

"Kamrie!" Mom's voice cheered. "Are you having fun? Tell me *everything*."

I smiled. "You mean is Tom Snow sexy in person? Well, I hate to burst your bubble, but—"

"Don't lie to your mother!" She laughed and the lucidity erased the tension from my shoulder blades, but put an ache of longing straight into my throat. "Tell the truth. I bet he's way nicer than his character. Although, that one scene where he pins his wife to the wall for one last round before the ink dries on their divorce? If I were younger, that man would be in trouble."

"Ugh, Mom." I groaned in misery but relished another hearty laugh in my ear, the normalcy I rarely experienced anymore.

"Kamrie, you know what I'm talking about."

"No, Mom, Detective Grayer is *your* favorite. I've only seen a couple episodes, so I don't know that scene. He claimed everything is all very professional."

"I don't know how actors do it," she said like we shared popcorn on the couch together. "The chemistry looks spicy on TV, but can you imagine having a whole audience while pretending to bump and grind?"

I cringed. "Can you not say bump and grind ever again?"

A sad sigh slammed my ear through the speaker. My heart clenched. Mom would never have sex again. Even if she wasn't promiscuous or married, I ached for what must be going through her mind in this sunset of her life. I moved the phone away from my face to retain my composure.

"Alright." I smiled, prayed she'd hear the cheer in my voice to lift her spirits. "You ready to hear about Tom Snow in real life?"

"Yes!" she gushed on the edge of her seat, her momentary grief paused. I imagined her sitting on the edge of her bed holding onto the handle of her walker rather than letting the home health nurse assist.

"He's—"

The phone yanked from my ear. I gasped and whirred around, ready to fight the creep from earlier. Tom Snow beamed and hit the speaker icon. "He's right here. This is Tom Snow. To whom do I have the pleasure of speaking with?"

My mouth dried and dropped open. I wasn't sure if I was more offended by the disruption or excited for my mom. When she cheered, I fought happy tears. She hadn't been excited in a while and I missed that sound.

"Tom Snow? *The* Tom Snow? This must be a trick."

He shook his head like she could see him. "No, ma'am. This is the real Tom Snow."

I imagined her frail fingers glancing her bony chest. "This is Evelyn Krouse."

"No shit?" Tom whispered to both of us. His eyes widened

and fell on my similar appearance like he suddenly saw me with glasses. "Young lady, *you* must be playing tricks on *me*."

Mom giggled and I swallowed my emotion as fast as I could. "Bless you, young man. No one's referred to me as young in a long while." *That she could recall, anyway.* "I'm her."

"If this is the real Evelyn Krouse, what was your outro for your morning newscast?"

Would she remember? Though I was miffed at the audacity of a stranger to steal my phone and conversation, I thrilled at Mom's once-upon-a-time, "Wishing you and yours a blessed day. Thankful for your views, this is Evelyn Krouse with channel forty-two, eye-witness news."

Tom sent me the genuine smile of a legit fan, then confirmed. "I'm a *huge* fan of your work, Ms. Krouse. My mom watched you every morning while I was getting ready for school. You were my first crush."

My pursed lips fell into a dumbfounded smile as a blush colored his stubbled cheeks when he glanced at me more like a nervous boy. He looked around us like he worried being found by a crazy fan of his own.

"I'm honored," Mom told him. "I'm a huge fan of yours. I asked my daughter to tell me if you were as handsome in person as your Detective Grayer character."

"What did she tell you?" Tom sent a shit-eating assurance my way. I rolled my eyes.

"She didn't."

"Should we put her on the spot?" Tom asked, his brows danced like a stupid teenager's, but I worried about our borrowed time.

I sighed and smirked, crossed my arms over my chest. "Hate to disappoint, but his makeup artist is a genius. I think he left her at the studio."

"Oh, Kamrie, you hush now," Mom chided like I were ridiculous.

"Kamrie? Like the car?" Tom teased. "Is that her name, Ms. Krouse?"

Mom giggled while my tongue traced inside my cheek. "Her name is *Kamryn*," I said and held my hand out for my phone.

He placed his hand on mine and twisted our palms so we shook. "Nice to meet you, Kamryn." He glanced around us again, and I realized if the creeper was still around, he'd know I'd lied if he heard Mom's voice on the phone. She could be talking to Tom from her room .... I prayed he wasn't lingering.

With my phone in hand, Tom walked toward the ramp. "My makeup artist is a man, by the way, and only Detective Grayer is a diva. *I* prefer a natural appearance when I step into the wild for these occasions, so where he's got shadows under his eyes and cheekbones, I'm sun-kissed. He's a nightwalker. I live by day."

I followed Tom's glance over his shoulder and Mom's answering laugh. "Is your daughter dating anyone, Ms. Krouse?"

"That's not your bus—"

Mom spoke over me. "Please, call me Evelyn. She's dated a few weathermen, a couple private investigators, oh, and there was a military man who had her heart, but we discovered he was having a baby, so—"

"Mom! Hush!" I jerked my phone from Tom's palm.

"Pregnant man, eh? Tough break," Tom continued, enjoyed Mom's laughter. "Weathermen get all the girls. If Kamryn watched the show, she'd know better than to date any type of detective." He winked at me. "Or military."

"They weren't weathermen," I insisted. "They were *meteo-rologists*. As in, out in the field. Not in front of a camera and green screen, thank you very much."

"Bummer." Tom snapped his fingers. "If there were no cameras involved, means they weren't even the cool storm-chasing type. Or attractive. Sounds boring."

I sent him pure annoyance, leaned my shoulder against the door to my room. "Mom, if you have any more questions for Tom Snow, now's your chance because I haven't eaten yet and hangry is about to happen."

"Kamrie Kole! You mean to tell me it's almost dinner time and you haven't eaten a thing?" Mom admonished me and I mentally facepalmed at my mistake. "Yes, I do have a question. Actually two for Tom."

Tom stepped closer like he wanted her to hear him better, but his shoulder rested against the door to my room, mirroring mine. The phone separated the inches between our chests. His cologne and fresh breath filled my space. I noted his tongue push a little mint into his cheek.

"I'm all ears, Evelyn. Your questions are likely better than the canned queries at these events. Wish you'd have been my interviewer. My mom would've flipped her sh— crap."

I fought a matching smile to his and threw the same poker face I'd worn during said interview.

"I'd have been honored to interview you, Mr. Snow."

"Please, call me Tom."

"Tom," Mom amended. "Will you please take my daughter to get something to eat? I need someone to make sure her blood sugar doesn't drop. She's diabe—"

"I'm not diabetic, Mom. I'm hypoglycemic. There's a diff—"

Tom waved his hand through my protest. "You've got it. What's the other question?"

"Take my number so you can call me when you're done and confirm without battling my daughter?"

Tom laughed while I groaned like an annoyed teen, but secretly I wondered if she'd even know who texted if he followed through. His phone rose and thumbs danced as he asked for her number. Okay, Mom knew her phone number. That was good. I sighed and listened to the pair of them banter like they'd been friends their whole lives. "Oh, before we go, will you give me Kamryn's number, too? This way I can check on her after I leave?"

My eyes bugged then narrowed at him getting his way, typing my number into his phone while he explained that his flight was early in the morning. I couldn't be too annoyed given that Mom remembered my number by heart as well.

"Where do you live, Mr. Snow?" Mom asked.

"Mom, that's too personal."

"Las Vegas."

She clucked her tongue. I snorted to myself, sent a sarcastic smile. I mouthed *Mom hates Vegas.*

"What a shame, eh, Mom? Guess he's not perfect after all."

Tom arched an eyebrow like I had to try harder than that.

"Everyone's redeemable, Kamrie. Men who have something great at home don't need Vegas." I heard her snicker. My tongue dipped the inside of my cheek again. "Are you dating anyone, Tom?"

I shook my head and mouthed that he didn't need to answer.

"I'm not." His satisfied sarcasm shifted his lips into a crooked smirk. "I'm definitely lacking. My whole family says I need redemption, so you may be onto something, Evelyn."

three

KAMRIE

TOM HELD my eyes for an inappropriate amount of time. Unwilling to back off, I stared back like he was barking up the wrong tree.

I lifted the phone near my lips. Tom watched like we'd met on a cheap hook-up app. I snorted, though a tumble between the sheets with a sexy actor sounded appealing. "I'm going to go eat, Mom. I love you. Make sure you let the nurse cook for you, please? Treat her the way you want me to treat Tom?"

She huffed against the speaker. The nurse called that she was already cooking and that Mom was being nice.

"You promise to be nice to Tom?" Mom asked. I didn't miss the stubborn edge creeping into her voice. The clock on the phone displayed after five PM. Mom was like Cinderella turning to a grumpy pumpkin by six-thirty these days.

"I promise, but only if *you* promise me you'll be nice to the nurse."

"Fine." She sighed again. "I promise. You?"

Tom hooked his pinky with mine holding the phone. "Ms. Krouse—*Evelyn*, she's pinky promising right now."

"Ooh, Kamrie, you're with a man? Is he handsome?"

Tears burned my eyes before I could hide my instant pain. Tom's play shifted into genuine sympathy.

"He's handsome, yes." I indulged her and brought a little smile back to Tom's face. Dammit. The damage was done. The dirty secret was out.

"He's not another weatherman, is he?"

"No, Mom."

"Does he have husband hands?"

"Husband hands?" Tom asked. I facepalmed and furiously waved my hand at Tom not to indulge her anymore.

"Mom, I—"

She interrupted before I could stop her. "Hands a woman could imagine being the only ones to touch her ever again. Men from Las Vegas don't have those."

My cheeks heated as my free hand tossed the air. How did she not remember who I was speaking to, yet recalled him saying where he lived? This damn disease made zero sense.

Tom decided not to take offense. "Well, I've never met someone with husband hands myself, but I am an investigator like Detective Grayer."

When she cooed, jealousy mixed into my embarrassment and sorrow. She remembered Detective Grayer over our conversations.

Tom ignored my inner war. "I'm not quite as handsome as that guy, but I try."

Mom giggled and I couldn't help a reluctant smile, though my eyes still clouded with unshed tears. I resented how Tom seemed to calm her where I always antagonized her once her normalcy expired. I prayed the nurse wouldn't have a bad night ahead of herself.

"Mom, the detective's gonna take me to dinner. You make sure you eat the food I had delivered for you." At this point, the mention of a nurse could set her into an independent rage. "The lady should be there to bring it to you so you don't even have to leave your bed. Have her put on the Detective Grayer series."

"Wow, Kamryn, perfect timing, she's right here."

"Ms. Evelyn, your sweet daughter already gave me all my instructions," the nurse said in the background. "Is your favorite still turkey and gravy?"

"Did Lori hire you?" Mom hung the phone up without saying goodbye. My head dropped in defeat. My *sister*. She thought my sister hired the nurse. My damn sister who couldn't be bothered to leave her life in L.A. to visit. Or, even to make a simple phone call. Who left me alone to face the demons that came out of Mom the further this disease progressed. I couldn't win.

"Hey." Tom's thumb caressed my bicep. My stomach dip-flipped at the intimacy. "My grandpa had Alzheimer's with dementia when I was growing up. He used to call us Nazis and thought he was a prisoner of war trapped inside our house. Called me a lot of mean names, said mean things. His favorite was *I'll knock the fire outta you, ya little shit.* Forgot I was his grandson. I get it."

"I hate that you do. I'm sorry." I looked up at him, desperate to put away my pain, unable to recompose myself.

"It was a long time ago. I'm okay. He's in a better place, memory intact, with my Gran."

"Tom, this was all very kind of you, but I can't go to dinner with you." I pulled the key card from my back pocket and slapped the plastic against the keypad. The light glowed red. "Dammit. What's wrong with this thing?"

"Did you put it next to your phone?"

"No. Hell, maybe? Who knows?" I tried again. Red.

"Here." Tom took the key and laid the card gently against the pad. The light glowed green and he turned the handle, pushed the door open. Of course the key would work for him. Just like Mom would remember everything to do with him. I rushed inside for the box of tissues before my mascara melted over my cheeks. Tom came inside the suite and laid the key on the desk near the TV, tapped so I'd see. The door slammed with a solid thud.

"I'm sorry." I blew my nose, hated breaking down in front of a celebrity of all people. *All these months I'd remained composed and this is where I crumble? With this man?*

I balled the tissue and tossed the trash toward the can I missed. "Whatever." With shaky hands I rifled through my small pantry in the kitchenette, ripped open a little rice crispy treat, and practically inhaled the sugar. "You want one?" I didn't give him the option, I tossed a treat he caught. "Dinner of champions, right here."

He thanked me and ripped the package. "Stake out food," he said after a bite, chipmunk cheek.

I nodded through chewing. "Astute observation."

"The wannabe storm chaser chases stories instead?"

"Something like that. Before the world went to hell."

His arms opened. I closed my eyes on a long, hard blink, then opened my shuttered view to his soothing offering. "When's the last time you had a hug?"

I swiped under my nose, shook my head. "I can't remember."

"That's not healthy."

I sniffled. "When's the last time *you* had a hug?"

He snorted, threw a thumb over his shoulder. "In the convention center. Why do you think I ducked into the first hall I could find? The distributor didn't mail the books in time. Empty hands wanting my attention? I needed air. This place is like a maze. Imagine my relief when I came upon the reluctant participant from the front row."

My chest filled with a deep breath that released between my lips. "You offended?"

"Not in the least. I meant what I said. I don't have to be everyone's cup of tea. Now, what're you waiting for? I got what you need," he finished with a character voice like a Brooklyn drug dealer.

A little laugh coughed through my reticence. "What the hell? Why not?" I walked into his arms and relished the strength in his biceps, the heat of his body, the sound of his heart beating beneath my ear, his cologne, how he didn't try protecting his white shirt from my makeup. Evidence of how hard he worked out for his role rippled beneath my fingers clinging to his back.

My gasp melted into a moan when his hands kneaded the tension beneath my shoulder blades like he supernaturally sensed I carried constant pain there.

"You're really tense," he said. "You work out?"

"Does lifting an old lady to give her a shower and change her diapers count?"

He rested his cheek against my hair and his stubble scraped my temple when he nodded. "Absolutely. There's no weight in the gym that compares. You're a veritable body builder. I'm out of depth, here."

I laughed against his shirt. "That's really kind of you. All of it. Thank you for talking to her. She usually holds her memory longer than that. Lately, it's gotten down to about ten minutes." I leaned back to look into his face so close to mine. "She really is an enormous fan of yours. I'm so grateful for your ability to make her laugh." He sent another sad smile. I shook my head. "Don't."

"What?" His brows dipped.

"Don't do that."

"Do what? This?" His fingers kneaded harder and I practically wilted.

"No."

He stopped.

"No!" I cried. "Keep doing that."

He chuckled, kneaded again.

"Thank you. I mean, don't look at me *that* way. I'm so tired of that sad smile. The pity party no one wants to join. My sister quit when it got hard. I was into something deep when I paused my cover to care for her. I've been reduced to freelance jobs writing small articles and editing columns for other writers. Life is on perpetual hold. Even my own sister refuses to help since she got slapped and told to go to hell. You could say my job gave me thicker skin. I've faced monsters far scarier than an old lady with a temper."

He hummed as his fingers crawled slowly down my spine until I arched onto the tips of my toes and gripped his back with nails like claws. "I can't!" I cried. "It hurts."

"You have large knots down here at the base of your spine. You desperately need a massage. Ever hear of self care?"

A bitter laugh joined the pain in my spine. "I'm on borrowed time, Tom. I can't get a massage. Hell, I'm afraid to take showers longer than five minutes. She sent me here in her place because she remembered the conference. She doesn't remember how old she is, but she remembered *this*? *You?* The conference host found out about our situation. I'm supposed to speak tomorrow to honor her career. I haven't told anyone I'm her daughter because I want to blend in without all the empty sympathy following me like a constant cloud. How can I speak to a crowd when I break down in front of an audience of one? I just want to go home."

"Where's home?" He eased his technique until I could

handle him rubbing circles into the places of pain like he could flatten them.

I laughed without humor. "Before or after she got sick?"

"Both."

"I was living in San Antonio, Texas. Now I'm in a little refuge of a town not too far from where you call home."

"Yeah? I like the sound of that." He changed from small circles to long, almost sensual strokes up and down my spine that pulled me tighter against him. "What's the town?"

"This perfect little place with perfect little families where nothing worse than teens toilet papering trees or taking potted plants seems to happen. Mom loves it. Well, she did before— oooh... keep doing that." I found myself rubbing the spot on his back I wanted him to rub on mine. A groan trapped in his chest vibrated mine. I swallowed and fought the attraction I didn't want to feel for him. "She forced me to go skiing with her last winter. The town during Christmas was like a Thomas Kincaid painting. The way they all come together to do holidays ... it's ... life isn't like that outside movies about writers getting trapped inside an inn that needs saving before Christmas if you get my drift."

Another hum vibrated through his chest to mine. "Sounds like something I wouldn't mind stepping into right now. Maybe a little Christmas in July action?"

I grinned against his shirt. "In the spirit of cliches, you could portray the famous actor seeking an escape from his popularity in a place where no one cares who you are, only that you join."

"You could be a baker. You smell sweet."

"Thanks. It's my perfume."

"It's your hair. Your skin."

I bit my lip. He was good. Especially the hands with the compliments? Why choose me? Was it the crush on my mom? My resemblance to her?

Tom snickered to himself. "San Antonio, Texas. No wonder you couldn't find any cool storm chasers. You have to hit at least Oklahoma to score a real adventure."

My hand ceased movement on his back as I leaned away to see him better, eyebrow arched in playful disapproval. I ignored the way his grip kept my hips against his. Tom's distinguished salt and pepper dashed with a daring youth deployed at the end of his serious news broadcasts. He wasn't the only one with a secret crush. I had a hard time watching Detective Grayer when the journalist was the one who'd held my attention. The fingers of my right hand inched up to the hair brushing his collar.

"How do you know about the storm chasing?"

He shrugged, sent another whiff of spicy cologne into seducing my senses. "Let's say, I understand the allure. The adventure. Reverence. A tornado is like love; a fearsome, fascinating terror. Hypnotic. Painful if you get too close. I don't think it was the weather geeks you were there for. They were the side show to your real attraction."

Tom licked his lips and I swallowed. Was that what I was there for? Some search for love?

"My freshman year in college, I was home doing laundry. Mom called me into the living room, said I had to see this new kid stealing hearts and her thunder. You were doing smalltime sportscasting in front of home team stadiums, making crowds laugh with your 'fan on the street' interviews. Instead of resentment, she'd pointed with her remote, said *this one's going places*. She always knew. Broke a few hearts with her honesty." I looked away from his pleasant surprise. "I wanted to be a meteorologist. She wanted me to study broadcast journalism. I hated being in front of the camera. She wanted me to carry her legacy because I look like her. My sister looks nothing like her, but she fell in love with acting and didn't want to sit at a desk. Now, Mom has no one to represent all she worked for."

His massage paused in lieu of pulling me into a tight embrace. I stood on the tips of my high heels. My arms wrapped harder around the back of his neck to reciprocate. How did this stranger provide more support than my last two relationships?

He pulled back enough to see me, and I lowered back to the height of my shoes. With the way he held me, I had the sudden longing to be kissed like a classic movie maven. Would he kiss with closed lips or tongue? Did he have the lizard tongue that darted in and out? Slimy?

"Life's not over."

I shook my head again. "No, it's not, but while my plans are paused, life spins too fast. I need it to stall with me, long enough to regain my bearings so I don't get dizzy. I'm tired of learning. Of thinking. Of pretending for the job. I need a break."

His turn to laugh without humor. "That, I can relate to."

"Oh?" I lifted my face to examine his again. His eyes traced what I guessed were the black streaks staining my cheeks.

"These authors with stars of hope in their eyes have no idea writing the book was the easiest part. They think these companies throw millions behind making you millions." He licked his lips again. "Nope. They keep their money for the authors who've made them money for decades. Their marketing plans haven't changed since the turn of the century and they simply erase the previous title and author name, insert yours. It's a machine. If I want Grayer to succeed, I create the marketing and pay for it with my advances. The negotiations for rights and royalties are so exhausting, the unglamorous bits kill all creativity. Then there's the drama on set."

"Such as?" I asked while he examined the couch behind me. Bad idea. Last thing I needed was to fall into some teenaged lust on those cushions with an actor leaving tomorrow. My fingers danced across the back of his neck to bring him back to me.

"Take my co-star, for example. Everyone talks about our

chemistry. Now I've got an earful about their divorce ruining one of the audience's favorite parts of the show, about why Detective Grayer has to be a shitty husband. *I* wrote the character. He does what I want. If I want him to get a divorce, he gets a damn divorce. If readers want a character to do what they want, then write their own stories, ya know?" I nodded and peeked at the stains I'd left on his shirt, felt a tad guilty. "Want to know a dirty secret?"

My eyes jumped back to his. I reached behind my back to link my pinky in his still-working hand, sent a small grin he reciprocated.

"You can't tell anyone."

"I promise," I said.

"I *hate* touching her and I hate kissing her even more. She has *the* worst breath. She got pissed when I asked her to use breath mints prior to our scenes. When she refused, I pulled the detective trick with mentholated salve under my nose, you know, like they use around dead bodies until they're seasoned? She said she didn't want to kiss someone with a cold. I told her I didn't have a cold, that I couldn't kiss her without the salve."

"Tom! You didn't!"

"I did. Honesty is the best policy. It's just business. She got so emotional, she hired a lawyer to sue for toxic work environment." He rolled his eyes. "Claimed my request is a result of toxic masculinity. I claimed it's common decency. She has no case, but the previous strain between us grew to unbearable. So, yeah, divorce. The producer is miffed. So are fans of us together."

My brows rose, lips puckered out of habit. "Yeah, Mom says everyone goes on about some spicy scene between y'all. One last time for the road?"

His head tilted back. A guilty smile erased most of his

feigned annoyance. He gazed back down at me. "Did she tell you about the nudity?"

Laughter erupted from my throat. I blushed and looked away, embarrassed. "No."

"Well, I'll be the first to tell you I'll take good breath over great boobs and a shitty personality. Every love scene was a true test of my acting ability."

My eyes traveled to the keycard resting upon the desk. His pinky linked in mine squeezed like he culled my attention. My chin lifted with my eyes. His hand ceased kneading my back and fingers instead threaded through the rest of mine in the hand behind myself. My thumb traced a callus on the inside of his palm; rough, warm, large. I swallowed and watched him do the same. His other hand rubbed slow circles up the center of my spine. When he reached my neck, my forehead fell against his chest. His fingers splayed to massage either side and my head reflexively fell back till he cradled the base of my skull. My eyes closed like a happy kitty greedy for every ounce of affection to my tense muscles.

"Too bad you're not the actress in your family," Tom said too close to my lips. The heat from his mouth spread warmth through my limbs and lower belly. "You have sweet breath." So did he.

"I just ate marshmallows in my treat, remember?" I smiled without opening my eyes. "If I'd eaten spaghetti before your interview, we wouldn't be having this conversation. I'd be just like your co-star."

"You're nothing like her." His nose brushed the side of mine and my lips automatically opened with a silent prayer for what should come next. "I love spaghetti, by the way."

I grinned brighter. "I don't do this."

"What?" His speech whispered against my lips like the ultimate torture.

"Let strangers seduce me."

He gave the softest, hypnotic kiss, and my knees turned to jelly. "We aren't strangers. I've met your mom. We're practically engaged."

I giggled and enjoyed another small kiss.

"Will you eat spaghetti with me?" He nudged my nose with his again.

"Later." I wrapped my hand around his head, pulled him to close the millimeters separating our warm lips. His groan vibrated my throat before his tongue massaged mine as his hold tightened and pulled me flush against him. I moaned and angled my head, wrapped my arm around his head to increase the sudden urgency building between us. *No reptile tongue! No slime! Great technique! Hallelujah!*

My shoes kicked from my feet. He chuckled as I shrank a few inches while he grew several against my stomach. I pressed onto the tips of my toes and urged him to kiss me harder, to follow me as I walked backward until the backs of my knees hit the edge of the couch.

To my delight, he lifted me and my legs automatically wrapped his waist. He gripped my thighs at the tops of my stockings, bunched my pencil skirt to my waist, cursed, mumbled something about only seeing garters in movies, all between hasty nips at my swollen lips and angle changes. Rather than take me down on the couch like I expected, he carried me into the bedroom. Instead of lying me on the bed, he spun me until my back pressed the wall. He used his hips to hold me while his fingers fumbled with the buttons on my blouse.

"You're so fucking sexy." His mouth mauled my throat and I felt the clasp on the front of my bra come loose. I squirmed against the thickness straining his jeans. My bare breasts fell free. His hands shoved the cups and cotton aside so I was bared to him. I ripped my hands from sleeves and reached for his head again. He cupped my bottom and lifted me higher against the wall. I held his shoulders, writhed with intoxicating incoherence he infused with every touch and taste driving me crazy.

"I always wondered what it'd be like to unleash this way on someone I wanted to fuck in real life. Always wanted to see a woman part her legs with these thigh-highs hooked to one of those belts. These panties have to go."

"Oh, gawd!" I moaned when his hand shoved the silk aside, fingers found the perfect place to massage inside me. His free hand cupped and worked one of my breasts. I desperately pulled his hair like reins for more of the flavor on his tongue, for him to soothe the aches breaking over every sexual place in need of his brand of bliss. "More!" I clawed at the lapels of his shirt and yanked so hard all the buttons flung to the floor. "I've always wanted to do that," I huffed.

"I've always wanted someone to do that."

"Please," I begged. "Please."

"So polite," he said between scrubs of his stubble against my face as our tongues tangled every spare second, his hands pawing everywhere, mine tearing his sleeves from his chiseled shoulders. He released his hold on me, inside me, and leaned away to free his arms, then ripped his undershirt over his head. Damn! "Definitely hotter in person," I said against his neck. I loved the hollow between his collar bones and the way his head fell back for me to kiss his Adam's apple. His hands braced the wall at either side of my head and he ground his hips the way I wished he'd do without anything between us.

With the same fervor I'd kicked my shoes from my feet, my bare heels desperately tried pushing his pants down his bottom. He chuckled under my mouth, then leaned away, all the while suspending me against the wall with his hips. I reached between us and fumbled with his belt, the button of his jeans, the zipper. He watched like he got off on the visuals of how he sprang free, how I grabbed him. I got off on the hiss and momentary toss of his head again, the thrust between my fingers until he became deliciously frenzied.

"Fuck it." He reached between us, ripped the silk panties in half, grabbed my hand around him and guided the tip of himself to my entrance. "You're so warm!"

"So are you," I breathed and snaked my hand from below to grab his shoulders while he shimmied to split my opening. The tip pierced and I bit my lip, clawed his skin, watched his muscles shift as his callused hands cupped my bottom to lift me higher.

"Relax," he said, lips caressed my sweating forehead, pecs brushed my nipples.

"Sorry," I mumbled, lids heavy, lips plucked by his during the slow, rhythmic push deeper between the apex of my thighs. "It's been. A while." Inch by slow inch stung my untouched insides.

"I love that." He nudged my nose with his, tugged my lips with steamy, open-mouthed kisses. My head slapped the wall, a loud cry burst between our kiss, when all at once he slipped well beyond my entrance deep between the suddenly slick walls of my insides. When I wrapped my arms around his neck, he said something like, "now we're talking," then smothered my cry with his hot tongue. When his taste buds coaxed mine, the ridges of his shaft razed my every tension to the ground.

Steamy sweat beaded over our skin as his hips flexed beneath my ankles gripping and spurring him for more and more.

"Harder! Please!" I begged and rode the turbulence of the soaring heights climbing my pitchy squeals. His hands were everywhere like they couldn't quit touching, pinching, massaging, gripping. My hands splayed in his hair and I drank his harsh grunts with my moans of his name. "Please, Tom! Oh, Tom!"

"Say my real name."

"What's your real name?" I gasped through wisps of breath. "Go to the bed. I want to be on top."

"Fuck yeah!" He grabbed my back so we wouldn't disconnect, then carried me to the bed, fell on top of me, rolled so I could sit up. "Damn, you're beautiful, Kamrie." He shoved the bunched skirt further up my waist so he had a full view of our connection, the lacy tops of the stockings, their hooks to the garter belt.

"So are you," I said in drunk lust, loving his low lids, the bite of his lip under his grit teeth, the harsh fingers digging into my hips. My palms splayed over his chest, knees gripped his waist and braced against the mattress, I leaned up so he could taste my nipples while I ground hard against the length I couldn't seem to get enough of. Sweat dripped into my eyes and wet my scalp. His hands left my hips and gripped my ponytail while he demanded in the gruffest tone that I ride him harder, to make my tits bounce harder.

Damn, I was a sucker for a guy who lost his couth in the throes of passion. The dirtier his vocabulary, the harder our skin slapped. The elastic around my hair split and flew somewhere in my periphery. His hands wound my tresses into pigtails he used like his own reins to coax my pace, then he'd tug me down so he could kiss me or suck one of my nipples into his hungry mouth. He broke his recent drink of my breasts and bucked me off him.

"Roll over." He rolled me to my belly. I felt the zipper on my skirt tug loose, the fabric shimmy over my bottom, helped him pull the piece away. His rough palms tore the silk scrap of my panties and tugged them away as well. "That's better." His fingers traced the garter belt around my waist, my bare bottom, the tops of the stockings. Then, like he could handle no more, he said, "On your knees." I did as commanded, then he knocked my knees apart with one of his. "Rest your face on the comforter." He pushed my hair over my shoulders.

I felt him lean toward the nightstand, heard the snap of a lid, arched deeper and sucked my teeth at the icy liquid dripping all over my back. A lid snapped again before his hot hands melted the chill across my skin as his rough palms smoothed oil into my aching muscles.

He gripped my hips, placed his thumbs over the painful knots I'd winced under earlier, pressed ultra hard, then entered me again. I squealed and caught my balance. Tom pinned my hips until I stayed put, then set a rhythm that matched the pressure he applied with his thumbs to the pain taking a back seat to the power of him inside me. I matched his slow pace, backed into him while arched like a cat, gripped the sheets and pillows near my face.

"You like that?" He dragged his hands in kneading motions once more. Funny, I couldn't feel anything but pleasure, almost like the pain I used to feel added to the intensity of the high he provided.

"Best fucking massage of my life!" I gushed against the blanket.

"Only *fucking* massage of your life?" I heard the hopeful smile in his tone, gasped when he reached one hand beneath me, to the apex of my parted thighs, massaged in ways I squirmed for more and less at once.

I panted against the comforter, closed my eyes to focus on the bliss breaking over my body. "Yes!" I lost all strength in my legs. Acute euphoria constricted him inside me, knees quacked, face went numb, though I screamed into the comforter. His other hand left my back and cupped my fevered cries.

"Easy, Kam." He leaned down over my back, breath bathed my ear. "We don't want someone to think I'm hurting you."

Nothing hurt. Absolutely. Nothing.

Until he resumed a tormenting pace inside me. Too much pleasure and sensation overwhelmed my depleted desire. Somehow he made me desperate for him to finish, something I'd never thought in my entire life. When I heard him groan and still, my knees collapsed. His body rested on top of me like the best weighted blanket. He didn't disconnect, rather he resumed the slowest pace while remaining pressed against my flesh. The dimming flame inside flickered into a renewed ache for more.

He rolled slightly onto his side, tugged my hip so I'd shift with him, then he rubbed my breasts using the same sensuality restimulating my insides.

I reached back for his head, brought his mouth to mine for sloppy side kisses. "This is amazing," I mumbled into his mouth. Tongue exchange. "Yes, only *fucking* massage ever."

He chuckled and disconnected our mouths to bathe and bite my shoulders with his tongue and scrapes of his teeth.

"I didn't know *this* existed." *Or that a guy could last more than a couple minutes! That I could climax during sex! That I could climax before him! More than once!*

"Mmm. Me either." He licked the side of my neck, pulled my earlobe between his teeth. When I arched into his touch, he rolled to his back and I remained on my back, lying on top of his chest, still connected in the most bizarre position I never knew existed. His knees lifted so I had no choice but to plant my legs on either side of them. He used of my hips to keep a steady pace. When his other hand dipped below the garter belt to tease the folds of our connection again, I felt I might surely die of orgasm.

"Damn, that feels so good! I can't last much longer," he confessed.

"I can't handle you lasting any longer! Tap out!" I tapped

the comforter and loved the laugher against my back. His hand left my nether region and grabbed my other hip.

"Sit up again."

I did as he instructed and learned another type of massage while I had another pony ride. He held my hips and worked me through my next climax, all while his thumbs rubbed the knots in my lower back.

"Shit!"

I caught myself when he bucked me off his lap, then I heard sharp gasps for air, felt the brush of his moving knuckles against my bottom as he coaxed himself to finish. Heard the pull of tissues from the box beside the bed.

"Damn, Kamryn." He breathed like coming off a sprint. "Come here." His hand wrapped my waist and he tugged me gently to the spot beside him, urged my head into the crook of his arm, shifted so our bodies pressed together. "You are ..." He smoothed hair from my forehead. "I ... haven't got adequate adjectives to describe."

"That was fun." I gave him a bright smile and loved his laugh, the little cough away from my face while he caught his breath, the continued rise and fall of his chest.

"Fun is definitely a good word. So is mind-blowing. Incredible. C'mon, writer. Let's dig through our thesaurus."

four

KAMRIE

I TRACED the lines of his muscles and rib cage with my index finger, grinned at his tickled flinches, the little dimple creasing his cheek and the laugh lines near his eyes.

"I'm not a fiction writer like most of this convention. Pretty adjectives don't typically have a place in AP style works."

"That's right. Storm chaser chasing stories instead. Tell me what you were working on before your mom got sick. You were in deep. Anything juicy?" He rolled onto his side to face me, so I adjusted and faced him, too. My lower lip sucked beneath my teeth when his index finger traced the curve of my hip up to the garter belt, toyed with the fabric.

I shrugged a shoulder. "Do we ever really stop working?"

He scoffed. "Fair point. You claim you quit working when she got sick."

"No, I paused deep cover."

"That's ..."

"Unwise?" I supplied, nodded. "It is, but I think the bait I was dangling wasn't working and the break works in my favor."

Tom's head fell back on a childish groan rather than the previous lusty ones. "You're killing me. What's the story?

36

What kind of lead can you sit on for, I'm guessing, months? A year?"

"Months. She's deteriorating fast. She hid her diagnosis for years until she could hide it no more. Can't dispute the call from the mental hospital after she was picked up by the police thinking she was a teenaged run-away. Begged them not to send her back to her parents." I glanced at the bed, drew invisible patterns in the comforter.

Tom leaned in for several kisses, then gripped my hip enough I cackled into a pillow and shoved his hand. "Come on, confession is good for the soul. You're getting it all out anyway. We don't even have a sheet between us."

Our eyes met, and though we were both depleted, resplendent with afterglow, a rekindling heat traveled between us. Never had I functioned on eye contact with someone who read my expression and instinctively knew what I needed, but never had I wanted to reciprocate and open up to another. Secrets paid my bills. Giving them away was like throwing money from a building. Something about Tom made me realize the heavy burden bottled inside, that I was tired of the game I loved.

"Let's just say if by some miracle I get to publish—" I caught his naughty hand before he could tickle again. "—I'd wreck Christmas for millions. I'll be lucky if anyone will be brave enough to buy it for more than killing it."

His brows dipped. "You writing an exposé on Santa? Gonna tell the kids the truth?"

I giggled, but my lips twisted to the side while I looked at the ceiling. "Something like that."

"Wait." He leaned up on his elbow for a better look at my face. "Are you *really* writing about *Santa*?" My head tilted in a more or less way. "Kamryn, I was kidding." Tom's eyes traveled my head like he searched for missing pieces to the puzzle of my brain.

"Tom, if ya know, ya know."

"What does that even mean?" He scrubbed his chin. "I know parents and grandparents pretend to be Santa every year. What else could there be? Can I read it? You talking publishing for a Christmas in July spiel? Or, are you waiting for real Christmas? Novel format or periodical? How big is this piece?"

I covered his mouth. "So many questions, so little finesse. Been outta the game for too long?"

His fingers threaded through mine before he unmuzzled himself. "You can't handle anymore finesse." He leaned up and attacked my neck with his mouth until I cackled and shoved him away again. His grin toned down and lingered on my face. "You're never out of the game, Kamrie. If you actually read my Detective Grayer novels, you'd see I hide true crime in the pages and mask them as fiction to keep my ass from cutting grass."

My brow arched. "You mean so your ass isn't grass?"

"No, I meant what I said. I don't want to be out of a job and forced to mow lawns like I did as a teen to make money. I write stories that haven't yet come to light. Things I've stumbled upon but don't want others realizing."

"As in, you've never stopped investigative journalism?"

"Astute observation."

I cackled at his sarcasm. "That's quite passive-aggressive, don't you think? The flaw with your method is that there's no breaking news. No interviews on the courthouse steps. No-one charged and brought to justice because of your work."

"Ever hear of *ripped from the headlines* crime novels?" His brows quirked, eyes lit with devious challenge. "Is the book ripped from the headlines, or are the headlines a result of work leaked after the book is written and ready to capitalize on a popular scandal that comes to light?"

I jerked back and gaped at him. "Is that how you play the popularity game?" He mocked my more or less head tilt, pretended to zip his lips. I lightly punched his shoulder. "Tell me! Is that how it works? Is nothing organic?"

He pushed me onto my back, climbed over me, settled his body between my knees. His chest rested on my pelvis while he looked beyond my breasts to my face. "Do you really think there are that many writers who blast eighty-thousand words within a week, editors who pull three rounds, formatting, book-in-hand within one month to capture the moment?"

I averted my eyes. He jostled my knees and watched my breasts shift with the current. I threw my arm across them. He whined and kissed the hollow between my hip and leg, caught my knee-jerk reaction in his strong hand to protect his head.

"For an investigative journalist, you're naive. I figured you might be used to disappointment in your fellow humans." His tongue dipped against my skin. I sucked my teeth. He pressed both my thighs into the mattress to keep me from injuring him. I felt his smile as his lips and tongue caressed my skin. "I also play a *master* interrogator on TV." I gasped when all at once he threw my thighs apart and dipped his kiss between them.

I grabbed his hair and moaned long and slow with the wet caresses between little questions about my work. My brain was too fuzzy to form coherent words other than the name of the saintly Santa I could prove was naughty behind the scenes.

He paused and our eyes met, his wide. "The Meyers Family charity?"

"Yes."

"Damn, Kamryn. You're not naive. You're ...." He swallowed what appeared to be nervousness. "You sleep with him?" I gaped with offense. Tom dipped his tongue, swirled against me, prevented my thighs from squeezing his head.

"No!" I shouted when climax fired through my core. Tom ripped his mouth away like I'd hit him with cold water. "No, I meant keep going!" His laugh vibrated against my flesh when he dove back in. "I mean! I mean! I mean!" I couldn't stop panting and battling against pleasure so acute the sensation bordered on pain. My hips wrestled away from his grip as my feet propelled my back from the mattress like he performed an exorcism. All at once, I dropped back onto the bed as all steam and strength left my body. He sat back on his feet, studied me. Though he seemed pleased to please me once more, concern collected with the worry in his eyes.

"No, Tom. I've never slept with him. I *can* get info from people without sex, ya know?"

He raised his hands in surrender. "I wasn't implying anything like that."

"You didn't have to imply. You just asked me straight up." I shimmied to sitting against the pillows and pulled one over my body.

Tom cupped his face and sighed, fingers dragged down his cheeks. "Don't do that, Kamryn. Like you have to cover up, like this was—"

"Tom, I don't do this." I pointed between us. "I already told you that."

"You're telling me you've never slept with someone for information?"

"Have *you*? Is that your regular MO? What *you're* doing in my room here and now?" I rolled off the bed and went to the bathroom, turned the shower on. "What're you looking for? Sources? Fodder for your next novel? I don't have anything for you, Tom."

"Kamryn, stop." He rolled out of the bed and dove for the door but I slammed and locked it before he could stop me. "Are you kidding? How could I be after your information when I didn't even know you or what you wrote?" He knocked. "Kamryn, please. This was fun. Let's not ruin it."

My fingers fumbled to unhook the stockings and garter belt.

"*I* didn't ruin anything!" I shouted over the sound of the spray, shoved the stockings off with my toes, no care for snags I caused. "*You* did! Nothing is organic. You said so yourself and you got what you wanted from me."

"I didn't say that! You did! This *was* organic!"

I ripped the shower curtain aside and hated the tears in my eyes. "Just leave!"

"What about dinner? You promised your mom. You need more than rice crispy treats. Don't make me tell her!"

I stomped to the door, grabbed the handle, opened wide on a man who blocked the threshold to keep the door open. My eyes narrowed. "Don't you *dare* bring my mom into this. If you text, she probably won't even know your name and number. I can't guarantee she saved it. You'll only confuse her."

"You're way too sensitive. You'd wreck everything that just happened over a damn lead you should leave well enough alone."

"I'm not wrecking this over a lead. I'm pissed you brought my mother into this."

"Bullshit. All was great until you saw my concern for you. Anyone could tell you what you're doing is dangerous. If your mom was in her right mind, she'd—"

The slap to his cheek cut the words straight from his mouth. "How would you know?" I demanded. Steam billowed around us and warred with the air conditioning from the bedroom. Tom frowned down at me and stepped forward. I stepped back, uncertain how he reacted when angry. He kicked the door closed behind himself. I wrapped my arms across my chest, prayed he wasn't a violent man, cursed my stupidity for cornering myself.

He cupped my cheeks with warm, soft palms. A stark contrast to the pink print I'd left on his face. Involuntary tears filled my eyes at the way he answered my anger with tenderness. I hated that I loved his hands so much, loved his concern, the way he handled my mother. "Listen to me, Kamryn. Show biz is filled with dark characters. I promised my mom I'd never make a deal with the devil, that I'd walk if he ever came to me."

My heart raced, breathing shallowed. "Elliot Meyers isn't in show business."

Tom snorted, thumbs caressed. "You're smarter than that. I think you know where the high donor class for his charity comes from. You, like the general public, think billions pour in from people rounding up their totals at cash registers for a month out of the year?"

No. Which was why I'd created a secret identity as an accountant and planted business cards in creative places. The last piece of my puzzle were the financial records.

I unwrapped my arms to pull his hands from my face, blinked the tears blurring my vision onto my cheeks. "I'm *not* naive, dammit." He was right. If Mom were in her right mind, she'd have hidden me in WITSEC for what I'd already acquired. Mom being out of her mind was the only reason I could still work under the radar while caring for her. While telling others I wasn't working.

"I wish you were," Tom said. *Me, too.* "My fear is that you already know far more than someone who loves their own heartbeat, more than the side that likes making a deal. I worry you may even know the side that made you briefly fear I might slap you back. *That's* why I'm pleading with you to stay away from him. You haven't published yet. It's not too late to let it go." His eyes searched my expression. I hadn't gotten to that phase yet, but his nervousness made mine fester. "I like you, Kamryn." He held my gaze with something far deeper as if to say *I could love you if you let me.* "A lot. You're like a magnet."

I averted my eyes before he broke my resolve. "Tom, you just said you didn't even know me."

He sighed and reached for my waist, tugged me against his warmth. His thumb did the classic movie tip under my chin thing I told Mom I'd never experienced in real life, and I couldn't help wrapping my arms behind his neck, though I was way shorter without my high heels now. His lips pulled gently at mine before he stood tall and guided my head to his chest. I toyed with the hair at the nape of his neck. His heart beat faster than before. Tom's fingers found my back muscles, kneaded. "The knots are gone," he said against my hair like we weren't both naked, that he hadn't developed the tools for another round. He stopped rubbing and settled for wrapping his arms around me in the same hug that started everything. "I'm begging you, Kamryn." His lips found my temple. "Don't make me miss you. I already hate that I'll miss you when I leave in the morning ... my life is easier without emotional attachments."

"Mine, too."

I already missed him, too. He had husband hands. The question was, did he use Mom's words about them to manipulate me into longing for him for the rest of my life? How could anyone *not* want someone to generously touch them the way he'd touched and tamed me tonight? I hadn't been slapped by Elliot Meyers because I hadn't yet met him in person, but while investigating him, I'd uncovered buried records of settlements seemingly made with victims of his temper or predation. If I could wriggle into his personal life as an attractive accountant, I could prove those payouts were then paid back to him by means of cashed out life insurance policies disguised as large contributions to his Christmas charity. In the past year, I'd traced erased profiles for women who'd made the mistake of becoming his mistresses. The internet always remembers, the digital footprint never truly vanishes.

"Please, Kamryn," Tom pleaded like he knew my thoughts. "Don't make me miss you *forever*."

My eyes closed. "Easy for you to say, Tom. No story, equals no paycheck. How can you ask me to stop doing what *you're* still doing?"

"Shhh." Tom kissed my forehead, lips lingered against my skin. The bathroom filled with steam so thick condensation beaded on his stubble and over our skin. "Have dinner with me," he broke the pregnant silence. "Let's shower, get dressed, leave our lanyards and identities behind."

I leaned back to see his demeanor changed, like he wanted one last amazing night with me before I was gone. I knew that look because I always looked at Mom the same way. I was just afraid and adrift enough in this feeling he gave, one I'd never felt before, to indulge in the same. I thought of my roommate back in San Antonio, the Naval officer, his battle stories, how he said you go out knowing you'll die and to make the battle worth the honor. To not publish and follow through with this story was to allow more women to die by Elliot's hands or the hands of whomever he hired to finish them when he'd tired of them.

Yes, I wanted my fling, a happy memory to take with me into battle. Someone had to stop the evil masquerading as altruism.

"Tom." I playfully tugged his hair brushing my fingers. "I love the thumb thing under my chin. I've always wanted that."

The wholesome smile that filled my TV screen, presented. He tipped my chin and kissed me again. When he stopped, I ordered him to do it again, loved his grin against my lips. I could forget food and drink him for sustenance. Who needed more than this to survive?

"What's your real name?" I asked between brushes of our tongues.

"Huh?" He pulled away. One brow lifted.

I rolled my eyes and stared. He didn't budge. "Don't bullshit me. You told me to say your real name. When things were hot and heavy."

Tom considered me for a long minute. "What's yours?"

Though annoyed by his non-answer, I said, "Kamryn Nikole Krause. My birthday is Christmas Eve. Mom wasn't exactly thrilled with having another baby, so she joked that Santa brought her coal for Christmas. She'd call me Kamrie Coal from the time I can remember. I changed the spelling and adopted it as my nom de plume so my writing wouldn't gain clout because of Mom's name." I peered up while he scrubbed a hand across his chin instead of tipping mine any longer. "Tom, I'm not going to dinner with you until you tell me your real name." If I might die, I was gonna die with his real name in my heart.

He licked his lips. "If I tell you, please, do not, under *any* circumstances, use it in public or reveal it without my permission. It's a safeguard for my family."

"I promise. Do I get to call you by your real name in private?"

A naughty gleam lit his eyes, frown twisted into a smirk. "I'd love that."

In person, he carried the distinguished air of a disciple who'd delivered the news in your front room for years; quite the opposite of the rugged, shadowed, crime-weary detective he played on TV. As I waited on bated breath, I wondered if he ever missed his role on the evening news. He looked like a Paul, Caleb, Matthew, Mark, or John. Not Luke, though.

"Brogan Slossel."

I blinked my shock, stumbled over my echo of his name. "Brogan?"

"Don't ask what Mom was thinking. Everyone in the family has a name that starts with B. I think she was low on options that hadn't been taken, so she made some shit up."

I caught a laugh in my palm. "I'm sorry," I said into my hand. "I'm not laughing at your name. It's kinda neat."

"Not the name you want to hear bringing your trusted news at night."

"But it could be a cool detective name."

He did my more or less head tilt thing. "Meh. Maybe."

"Since I'm all Ks, guess we can't get married one day," I blurted and smothered another laugh to cover my embarrassing diarrhea of the mouth. He reached down and tickled my ribs, his laughter joining mine, though I believed his was probably from relief.

"Alrighty, Brogan Slossel." I offered my hand. His smile brightened as he shook my offering. "It's wonderful to meet you."

"Likewise, Kamryn Kole Krause. Don't worry, I can't bring the KKK home to Mom. You're safe."

I shook my head in disapproval. "Technically, it's KNK. And, we both know I can't bring a Vegas boy home for dinner."

"Good thing I'm leaving in the morning." He lifted me so my legs wrapped around him again.

"True story." Our lips met. "You're irredeemable."

"If I weren't, you wouldn't have as much fun." I grabbed his head, threaded my fingers through his hair. He walked me under the shower spray and held me tighter when I winced under the shock. "Grab that soap and cleanse me of my sins."

Hard to do when we couldn't quit sinning again.

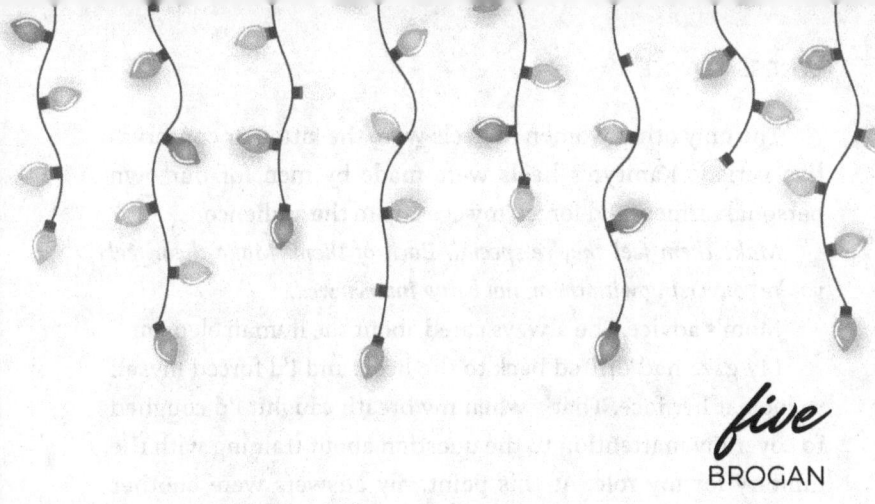

NEVER FALL IN LOVE. *It's a career-ender for attractive actors. If you want to make it, your only love is the industry.*

A career-ender. That's what Kamryn Kole was, this woman I couldn't quit kissing. The first girl I'd kissed without a role between us since I could remember.

I understand if you need a hook-up. Do what you have to do to grease the wheels, but no public dates. Your fans want to feel they have a chance, the illusion of hope, to be with you. The moment they see you with someone, you kill their dreams, ratings drop, so do royalties and roles. I like getting paid. You like getting laid. Keep it simple. Keep the flow. We're good to go.

My agent's advice beat through my brain as I redressed while I watched Kamryn pull black stockings over her pretty legs. She fastened the garter to the lace adorning her thigh, then shoved her foot into the same high heels that earlier caught my fancy from the front row. Had she twirled her toe to hypnotize me during my interview? I couldn't concentrate. Most writers wore jeans, Crocs, Hey Dudes, comfortable cotton emblazoned with names of past conventions, their brand, whatever they felt like.

The only other women in heels wore the kitten or conservative variety. Kamryn's heels were made by men for our own personal torment. I'd forced my eyes up to the audience.

Make them feel they're special. Each of them. Make them feel you're conversing with them, not being interviewed.

Mom's advice. She always cared about the human element.

My gaze had drifted back to the heels and I'd forced myself to look at her face. That's when my breath caught. I'd coughed to cover my inattention to the question about training with the military for my role. At this point, my answers were another role. Tom Snow was a character. That woman stood out like a lily among brambles; scripture my brother used to define his wife at their wedding. In my head, I heard him reciting his vows to her while the lines I'd said a hundred times flowed forth from my mouth. The audience laughed, so I knew I was on the right track. I couldn't stop my gaze from drifting back to her. Were my eyes playing tricks on me? She looked so much like the legendary Evelyn Krouse, I wanted to stop the interview and ask about her.

My agent's head turned, so I stood to pace the stage, steal his attention from what had mine. The woman didn't raise her hand as an eager participant. Because she didn't already have my intrigue. That toe spun circles while she fidgeted with her lanyard like I made her squirm in kind. Was I? Causing her to shift around that way? Did I want to?

Yes. I wanted to make her squirm on my lap. I swallowed and decided to end this early. Writing advice. That's what they all wanted. I'd just as soon remove my clothing, toss the threads into the audience, tell the few who'd caught them that the ratio of millionaires and overnight success stories were like the few among the thousand who worked just as hard without more than pennies on the dollar to show for their efforts.

My agent flared his eyes and I told them to just write the

damn books. You can't edit what doesn't exist. Why complicate matters? They were professionals. They weren't any less than me. I drew the lucky straw was the only difference.

"It's not the only difference, Tom," my agent griped in the corridor on the way to the signing area. "You can't teach talent. Not everyone has it. They can all type, but I guarantee not everyone out there is a writer, and—"

"I gave them hope, Jordan. People need hope. What did you want me to say?" We rounded into another empty hallway and ducked into a private elevator.

"I wanted you to tell them to get honest feedback. They came for professional advice and you spoke like they were hobbyists."

My hands tucked into my pockets. "They need to keep their love of the craft or else they'll lose their edge. I don't know what you're so upset about. They clapped at the end. They participated in all of my questions. I had their attention and kept it."

He smacked the button we'd failed to press in our staring contest. "Did you see the audience? You fool. You asked them who was a fan of your work. You removed the illusion that everyone in there was a fan. Your rankings will likely drop. Your publisher is likely flipping their shit."

"Big deal. The show ranks in the top ten."

He held his waist and pointed at nothing with his free hand. "The show is nothing without the novels, Tom. The novels are nothing without the show."

"Excuse me?" I demanded, affronted. "That show wouldn't exist without the popularity of the novels. I worked my ass off to write those books. I pay for the marketing."

He glared, cheeks covered in red splotches, humorless laugh snorted from his nostrils. "That show wouldn't exist without me working my ass off to get your books in front of a producer."

"You wouldn't have anything to peddle to producers if I

didn't write it, same as every damn one of those writers out there. What's wrong with the truth? Don't you think they need to know the hardships that come with the fame? The price you pay to see your characters come to life on a screen? I wish someone had told me. I might've never written."

"That's your problem, Tom. You're burnt out. Uncooperative."

"Uncooperative?" I couldn't believe my ears. I balled my fists inside my pockets. "All I've done is cooperate with your every booking, signing, lecture. Yeah forgive me if I'm burning out because you're burning my wick at both ends! I haven't had a day off in over two months." I threw a hand between us. "Don't even tell me that's the nature of the business. I already know. Remember where I started."

The doors parted. He opened his palm and gestured I exit ahead of him. "Never give up the illusion, Tom. Button up your bitterness. Have I taught you nothing?"

Our faces cleared of anger and we plastered smiles for the line of readers and writers eager for my autograph. Was the woman with the stilettos in the mix? A nervous pair rushed up to us.

"There was a problem with the shipping. The distributor pulled their tables from the event because they've screwed up so bad they can't take the heat. It's not just Tom's, it's every author whose publisher uses them."

"What does that mean?" Jordan barked.

I gave one of the helpers a sad smile, then cast a warm one to the line. "It means they have no books. Nothing for me to sign." My attention returned to the helper. "Do they know that already?"

"They do."

Jordan's face snapped toward the other helper's. "You mean they're here anyway? Not angry at us?"

"They're not angry. We've limited them to three of their personal copies. Mr. Snow, if you'll be seated, we only have twenty minutes until the next panels begin."

My butt hit the seat and I used my teeth to pull the cap from one of the five markers on the table. I signed worn paperbacks, coffee-stained hardcovers, the backs of grocery receipts, but the event program caught my eye.

The lady laid the pages open on my table, flipped, apologized for losing her place. I caught sight of Evelyn Krouse's headshot. My hand blocked the page from turning. "Mind if I see this for a second?"

"Oh, not at all, but your picture's on the page before this one."

I spun the program and read Evelyn Krouse's little bio, saw where she was slated to be a guest of honor at the conclusion of the event. The lady tapped Evelyn's image. "I heard her daughter is here in her stead, that she's the spitting image of her mother."

"Do you know why Evelyn isn't here?"

She shrugged. "No one has given specifics, but I think she's sick."

I frowned. "That's sad. I'm a fan."

"Oh, me too. I loved her interviews. She never let her guests get too serious. Like Joan Rivers meets Diane Sawyer. Just enough humor to keep from hurting feelings, pretty enough to be a beauty queen. If her daughter looks just like her—"

"I'm sorry, ma'am," Jordan interrupted and waved me on.

I ignored him and flipped to the page before Evelyn's, to my own image and biography. "If her daughter looks just like her, I'm in danger of losing my heart because Miss Evelyn was my first love. What's your name, gorgeous?"

If Jordan had hair on his shiny head, he'd have clawed it out. Hmm, maybe he had hair once upon a time and I'd caused his balding? I took a small satisfaction in that idea, even if it wasn't true. It could be.

I winked up at the lady before scrawling *Thanks for your support, Maria. Stay beautiful! - Tom Snow AKA Detective Grayer*

"Oh, my! Thank you, Mr. Snow."

"My pleasure."

"May I have a picture?"

"Absolutely." I smiled beside her while Jordan's lips thinned to a line in the sand between us. I smiled for photos, fought off a few inappropriate gropes, all while sending Jordan smug smirks in between. The line seemed to grow instead of shrink. Jordan checked his watch for the thousandth time, then stepped in the way of the table.

"I'm afraid that's all the time we have for now. Tom's window is closed."

By the time I was certain he was apologizing for the distributor's mistakes, I was gone, rushing for a place to hide from him more than the few fans who caught me in passing. I paused to smile in their selfies, thanked them when they gushed about the show, Detective Grayer, even asked me to sign his name to their phone case instead of Tom Snow. Fine by me. I tucked the stolen marker back in my pocket and trotted down a set of stairs, considered hopping into the gondola loading with tourists eager to take a trip on the manmade waterway bleeding into the arteries of the expansive resort. My brothers flitted through my imagination, how we'd have likely pushed each other into the water as kids, how Mom's angry outburst would've echoed off the glass ceilings of this atrium. Dad in his quiet disapproval would've probably gotten into the little boat and sat for his tour while we wrestled it out. Our sister complaining about us always embarrassing her.

From the lower level, I glimpsed Jordan's shiny dome

coming down the distant escalator, his head turning this way and that like he needed to find his lost dog, hook me back on a leash, cage me in the kennel so I wouldn't get stolen by someone with a better offer.

I rushed through the first set of double doors I glimpsed, apologized to a couple I'd nearly knocked down.

"Was that?" the woman asked, clearly not an attendee to the writing convention.

"Detective Grayer?" her husband finished her question.

"Nope. I get that everywhere." I waved over my shoulder.

The halls of rooms all looked the same, and, apart from that couple, were blissfully devoid of activity outside the house-keepers working down the way. I rushed that direction, prepared to hide behind one of their large carts if Jordan somehow tracked me. Hundreds of rooms. The maps at the ends of the halls I turned showed what a maze this place truly was. Sure, I was lost, but all halls had a guide for the restau-rants, shoppes, convention halls. Did he have tracking on my phone? Was there a way to check?

Damn, I'd lost my edge. Ten years ago, I'd have learned how to hack my device out of sheer stubbornness.

I rounded into another hallway, but stopped short. My breath stuttered. The woman with the shoes! Damn, she was sexy. Those stilettos crossed now at the ankle, her calves checked tight, the little slit in the back of her pencil skirt, fabric hugging round hips ....

The point of her shoe drew circles like she might do the same with her bare toes in the carpet if she removed them. Her wavy ponytail shifted when she leaned to look down the hallway like she was hiding from someone as well. Her phone met her ear.

I smiled when I heard the smile in her voice. A pleasant

voice. Not too high, not too low. I willed myself to play it cool when I heard, "You mean is Tom Snow sexy in person? Well, I hate to burst your bubble, but—"

My neck twisted as I checked for housekeeping or others in the hallway who might catch me spying on her. How to talk to her without coming off creepy?

"Ugh, Mom." She groaned more like a teen girl teased about the boy she liked. Did she like— "No, Mom, Detective Grayer is *your* favorite." Guess I had my answer. Can't win them all, but if Evelyn Krouse was on the other end of that call, who else did I need to win? There couldn't be a higher honor. I listened as she continued. "I've only seen a couple episodes, so I don't know that scene. He claimed everything is all very professional."

Ah, *the* sex scene. I nearly shuddered at the memory of take after take with Ana's breath in my face.

The woman's hand fanned into a stop sign. "Can you not say bump and grind ever again?"

I fought a laugh.

"Alright. You ready to hear about Tom Snow in real life?"

I sure was. Maybe. Nope. She might say something awful and kill my spirit. I pushed off the wall.

"He's—"

Before I harnessed my poor manners, I stole the phone from her hand like I could command the same attention she'd demanded from me earlier. She gasped and spun on that stiletto like a sexy ballet dancer. I grinned like Detective Grayer does at perps behind bars. "He's right here," I said to the prettier, non-eighties and nineties version of Evelyn Krouse. An updated model. "This is Tom Snow. To whom do I have the pleasure of speaking with?"

Please say Evelyn or else I'm better off finding Jordan and getting in the kennel.

"Tom Snow? *The* Tom Snow? This must be a trick."

"No, ma'am. This is the real Tom Snow."

I knew before she confirmed, "This is Evelyn Krouse." If I made anyone else feel this giddy, I couldn't imagine.

"No shit?" I blurted and overtly checked her daughter out like I'd stumbled upon the ultimate set of fantasy twins. How complicated. Must separate them in my brain. "Young lady, *you* must be playing tricks on *me*."

My palm holding the phone tingled at the ability to make Evelyn Krouse giggle. Her daughter, on the other hand, seemed emotional. Was she truly mad at me for stealing her phone?

"Bless you, young man. No one's referred to me as young in a long while. I'm her."

"If this is the real Evelyn Krouse, what was your outro for your morning newscast?" I enjoyed the reluctant smile from the poker player studying my facade for tells and chinks in my armor. Evelyn indulged me with her signature exit lines and the words were like chicken soup on a sick day. I was immediately transported into the living room, Mom folding loads of laundry, chiding the five of us to finish getting ready for school.

Unable to help myself, I did the thing. I gushed about what a fan I was, caught the woman relish the heat hitting my cheeks. I peeked around for Jordan. He seemed to have an innate ability to ruin special moments, and this one was such he probably felt my happiness like a homing beacon.

"I'm a huge fan of yours," Evelyn said. "I asked my daughter to tell me if you were as handsome in person as your Detective Grayer character."

My stomach flip-flopped. "What did she tell you?"

She rolled her eyes at me.

Evelyn said, "She didn't."

It was like the high school version of myself presented before a pretty face and I couldn't help becoming a flirty idiot. "Should we put her on the spot?"

She sighed and her arms crossed over her demur blouse. Pft. That top was like covering a Ferrari. A man didn't need to know the model, he could tell by the shape she was sure to be sheer beauty when bared to the light of day. The woman smirked like she knew I imagined her topless.

"Hate to disappoint," she said, "but his makeup artist is a genius. I think he left her at the studio."

Ouch! I play winced. If she'd thought me unattractive or annoying, she'd have put that stiletto up my ass.

"Oh, Kamrie, you hush now," Evelyn said.

"Kamrie?" I licked my dry lips, feeling a tad caught in my naughty metaphor. "Like the car?" Toyota wished they made something this pretty. "Is that her name, Ms. Krouse?"

She giggled and her daughter's tongue lined the inside of her cheek. Blow jobs. Yep, I'm screwed.

"Her name is *Kamryn*," the woman stated like she might put that stiletto in my heart if I didn't quit thinking with the wrong head. She opened her palm. Without thinking, I took her hand and gave a firm shake to show I wasn't meaning to offend.

"Nice to meet you, Kamryn."

My phone vibrated in my back pocket. If I didn't get out of here, Jordan would track me. I sensed him like the dog he treated me as. He was close. I walked toward the end of the hallway, glimpsed the convention hall floors. I gave the woman no choice but to follow my lead. "My makeup artist is a man, by the way, and only Detective Grayer is a diva. *I* prefer a natural appearance when I step into the wild for these occasions, so where he's got shadows under his eyes and cheekbones, I'm sun-kissed. He's a nightwalker. I live by day."

I paused before the ramp and tiny staircase beside it, twisted to face Kamryn. Rebellion took root. "Is your daughter dating anyone, Ms. Krouse?"

Kamryn's jaw dropped. "That's not your bus—"

"Please, call me Evelyn. She's dated a few weathermen, a couple private investigators, oh, and there was a military man who had her heart, but we discovered he was having a baby, so—"

"Mom! Hush!" She yanked the phone from my hand. My time was almost up. If I didn't make Kamryn laugh, I wouldn't have a shot. If Jordan found me, I'd have even less.

"Pregnant man, eh? Tough break," I joked. "Weathermen get all the girls. If Kamryn watched the show, she'd know better than to date any type of detective." I winked at her. "Or military."

Her face twisted into skepticism, the type that said I didn't have a chance in hell.

"They weren't weathermen. They were *meteorologists*. As in, out in the field. Not in front of a camera and green screen, thank you very much."

In other words, unattractive or dorky. I couldn't help spelling as much, knocking the cock out of her walk. How did she walk? I didn't get to see her walk away, but I didn't want her to. Damn, what a mess.

Then, the subject of food came up and I had my in. If this woman was hypoglycemic she might not be a bitch, just hungry. I couldn't help praying that Evelyn Krouse didn't raise a self-important snob. I was losing hope, getting ready to book out and keep running from Jordan when Evelyn asked if her daughter was with a man, if he had husband hands.

My attention riveted on the sudden sorrow in the woman before me and I knew she had more heart than she wanted to. Her mask was like my own. Evelyn Krouse wasn't sick with cancer or a cold. She had Alzheimer's and her daughter was a mess melting before me. To my surprise, she produced a key card for the door we both leaned against at the mouth of this hallway. Of course the convention would've given Evelyn the closest room.

Jordan's shiny dome caught the light. I grabbed the keycard from Kamryn's shaking hands, worried she'd demagnetized her card by placing it by her phone. We both seemed relieved when the light glowed green. I ducked into the room after her. She apologized, beelined straight for the tissue box, blew her nose in a very human moment that brought her down to an approachable level. She balled the snot wad and aimed for the trash can only five feet away from her, missed, muttered under her breath. More human points.

I laid the card on the desk. If Jordan spied me dipping into this room with a woman, I expected a knock to follow us any second. I watched the entrance, then my attention shifted to Kamryn's hasty reach for rice crispy treats. One burst from the wrapper so fast, she caught it before it flew to the floor.

Jordan's muffled voice leeched through the door. "No, I can't find him. I think his battery is dead. He never charges his damn phone. Well, that order will be too late. He has a flight at four AM. The distributor needs to get their shit together."

"You want one?" She chucked the sugar cube with poor aim. I caught it to keep her from crying. The tears caught me off guard. If she didn't slow her roll, the Ferrari would be as easy to take for a spin as the Toyota. "Dinner of champions, right here."

"Thanks." I shoved a large piece in my mouth, remembered myself too late. "Stake out food." I was the Toyota now.

"Astute observation."

My brow furrowed for a beat. Had I said the Toyota bit aloud?

Jordan's voice drifted down the hallway and I relaxed. My phone wasn't dead, but maybe I didn't have good service in this room. Was there a better place to be? Trapped with the woman of my teenaged dreams, or at least the updated version, no cell service, no one knowing where I was. I focused on the black streaks dried on her cheeks.

Toyotas are pretty, too.

"The wannabe storm chaser chases stories instead?" I offered.

"Something like that. Before the world went to hell."

What do you say to someone who's losing their parent? My grandad was like a living dead man. A stranger. Death would've been easier than having him reject you before passing. Unable to offer anything else, I opened my arms to her.

"When's the last time you had a hug?"

She looked at me like I was crazy, wiped her nose with her hand, and shook her head. "I can't remember." The sexy siren lost her supernatural quality and where I'd taken pleasure in her humanity moments earlier, I now hated seeing the power leeching from her like a Phoenix losing the ability to fly.

"That's not healthy," I said more to my thoughts.

"When's the last time *you* had a hug?" she asked.

"In the convention center. Why do you think I ducked into the first hall I could find? The distributor didn't mail the books in time. Empty hands wanting my attention? I needed air." I omitted my possessive agent putting me into submission. "This place is like a maze. Imagine my relief when I came upon the reluctant participant from the front row."

Her chest rose and the Ferrari's shape was undeniable. "You offended?"

Pft! "Not in the least. I meant what I said. I don't have to be everyone's cup of tea." I wanted to be hers if only for an hour. "Now, what're you waiting for? I got what you need." She needed a lot more than a hug.

"What the hell? Why not?"

Her perfume smelled like vanilla and orange blossoms. My heart rushed blood from my head to south of my border as she pressed herself against me and gripped my back in ways I wanted to make her nails dig as I made her scream with pleasure.

It wasn't enough to hug her. I had to hear what her moan would sound like. I'd never had a massage that didn't make me moan when the masseuse hit the spots where I carried my stress.

six

BROGAN

NOW, she knelt and pulled the other stocking up her leg and I found myself reliving the flavor of her breath and skin, the feel of her wrapped around my again-pounding head, the view of her bent forward while I finished harder than I had in the longest.

Her other foot fit into the matching stiletto. I liked that she didn't bother drying her hair. Even though she had the eighties waves taking over without tools, her mother's hair, I no longer had a crush on her mother or her resemblance to her. I'd scratched the itch, banged the prettiest woman at the convention, but instead of leaving, I found the same magnetic pull keeping me grounded to her presence. The fuck if I knew why I wanted to solve her sadness, to make her laugh, to touch her in a way she'd want to be touched the rest of her life. I didn't want to be a husband.

Did I? Was I having a mid-life crisis? What evoked this chaos?

I couldn't even tuck my tail between my legs, drag back to Jordan's door and tell him I was ready to leave, that I'd felt the call, followed the scent, had my fix. Kamryn and I just had round two in the shower and it was like she'd taken the leash from Jordan, from my ambitions, relieved me of duty if I'd like to sit by her side and keep guard, wait obediently for treats and a pat to my head. I wouldn't mind more scratches to my back. The business with Elliot Meyers made me want to lie down in front of her door to keep anyone from coming through to hurt her. That story, the way women disappeared around him, could easily get her killed.

Kamryn stood and finger-fluffed her hair. The idea of Elliot trying to touch her, and what he would try if she kept going, made me sick. She was special. A pretty woman with a heart big enough to pause her life and play full-time nurse to a mother vanishing before her eyes? Was that why I fixated? Like if she was only pretty I could leave satisfied?

You never break someone with a heart, Brogan. There are heart-breaks in life, but most stem from selfishness. You never break a heart that has a heart for others.

My mother's wisdom, the small things she'd say when she probably thought we weren't listening, played through my mind around her. While Evelyn's memory of Kamryn would likely fade, I desperately longed to see the mother who'd never stopped praying and hoping for me to be a good man like my father and my twin brother.

"Hey, Kamrie."

"Yeah?" She paused with her blouse in hand, wearing nothing but stockings, the garter belt, pretty panties, and a lacy bra. Kamryn looked up at me. I snapped a photo on my phone.

"Confession time. I want you to leave the skirt and heels here. Take that formal stuff off. Put on jeans or sweats. Yoga pants if you're feeling mean. Panties optional."

Her hair tossed with her head on a laugh. "Come again?"

"That's the problem, I don't have time and we have to eat."

"Brogan." She tsked and dropped the blouse on the bed. "You want me to change again? After all that work?"

Brogan. So natural. Like to her Tom was also just a character. Did telling her my name cause this problem? This loyalty?

I play-winced. "I only wanted to watch you put them back on. Now I want to watch you take them back off. Please?"

She put her dainty fists on her hips, wry grin flavoring her sarcastic smile. I put my phone on video and leaned into the frame with her in the background. "This is Brogan Slossel coming to you live with journalist Kamryn Krouse. Oh, yeah, she hides from the camera, but she can't hide from mine. Kamryn, inquiring minds want to know, did you really cause Tom Snow to walk away from his role as Detective Grayer?"

She gasped, asked what the hell I was talking about.

"Well, I'm not sure how to pretend with anyone after being too real with you," I told her, leaned in for a kiss. She smiled and pushed the camera away. I looked at the camera. "Guess this means I'll have to write a sexy affair with an investigative journalist for Grayer. Get you to audition for the role."

"Oh?" She walked out of the frame and rifled through her dresser. Of course she was the type to unpack her suitcase and live in the room. She shoved her feet into a pair of yoga pants she pulled up tight over her silk panties, shimmied past to torment me, sly grin over her shoulder.

"When you become famous, fans like to know who you are when you're not playing the role that twists Detective Grayer around your finger. Tell us what Kamryn Kole is like? What does she do in her spare time?"

Kamryn giggled. "Well, unless I just played a role with Detective Grayer, I haven't twisted him around my finger just yet. I've twisted Brogan Slossel around my finger, perhaps Tom Snow, too."

"Semantics," I joked to the camera. "Typical reporter. Quit dodging the question."

I heard her snicker. "She hates jogging but it's the cheapest high around," she said and slipped into a convention t-shirt. I couldn't help my disappointment. Her long hair tied into a sloppy bun on top of her head. "Let's see." She bit a bobby pin in her mouth, spoke through her closed lips. "She forgets to shower and eat when she's on the hunt. Basic hygiene is a problem." She winked at the camera, kissed my cheek. "Sometimes farts in public because she's so used to being alone she doesn't have to think about it."

My phone came down while I laughed my shock. I lifted the camera again. "If you like cars and football, I'm gonna propose."

"Nah, uh. You can't propose. My name doesn't start with B."

"Oh, that's right." I paid attention to my pretend audience again. "If I were living to please my parents, I'd have placed a prerequisite on dating a woman with a B name. I'd have also surrendered to the ministry and be preaching like my Pops."

Kamryn jumped into the frame, but stared at me. "You're a PK?"

"Preacher's kid? That I am, Special K." I grinned at her, kissed her, then grabbed the back of her head to force her to kiss me for real on the video. Her hands in my hair, the nails curled into my scalp, I couldn't get enough of that passion. When she broke the kiss, I tugged her back, caught her chin under my thumb, loved how she lost her fight against affection on camera like I'd pushed a compliant button in that single motion.

She walked out of the video, said she was hungry. I begged for one selfie and loved when she tucked under my arm and smiled up at the camera beside me. I snapped another with me kissing her cheek, then tucked my phone back into my pocket. This way I could take her with me on the road.

I saw her grab her phone a moment later, grin at the images

I'd sent her. "For you to remember me by when morning comes and you discover you've lost a shoe."

"Lost a shoe? Like Cinderella or something?"

"Ish. More so because I'm a pervert and wanted a souvenir."

She cackled and tucked her phone into a front pocket.

"Airplane mode for you." I thumbed the feature on my phone, ignored the incessant notifications from Jordan. At least this way, he couldn't interrupt our dinner. My hand wrapped the door knob. Kamryn displayed her phone and tapped airplane mode, too, but sudden guilt stole her happy smile. Evelyn. "Hey, Kam. Keep your ringer on. She might need you. No one needs me like that, so I have the luxury." Even as I said the words, the sentiment soured in my mouth and Kamryn sent a modicum of pity my way. Even as I knew she likely longed for the easy days of just being a daughter to her mother, longed to quit changing diapers or doing battle, she was needed. No one needed me. Except Jordan. To pay his gambling debts. He couldn't hide his unsavory habit from a professional investigator.

"I'm sorry, Brogan." She looked up at me with a plea in her eyes. "You know I'd do the same if I could, right?"

My thumb brushed her chin. "I do now and I'm honored." The tension and sorrow fled from her frame anytime I cupped her cheeks or tipped her chin under my thumb. I loved her reaction to my simple touch.

"If you don't stop doing that, there will be no dinner." Her pretty eyes crinkled with another smile. "I'll hold you hostage, force-feed you rice crispy treats, and make you give me your special massages with happy endings until you have to leave, but I won't let you leave."

My head fell back while I stomped my feet and threw a mini tantrum that I couldn't do all of the above. She clapped and laughed before opening the door. I walked into her back as she stopped in her tracks.

A furious bald bastard bent on banishing me to my room leaned against the opposite wall like he had all the time in the world. His arms crossed over his chest, tight frown on his face.

"Two words," Jordan spat, his hand displayed two fingers.

Kamrie asked, "Can I help you?"

Jordan looked through her. "One starts with a C, the other an E."

"He's my agent," I told her.

Jordan pushed off the wall and wiggled his phone. "He's also been looking for his missing client for hours. If you weren't so selfish, you'd remember you promised to do a private reading from the first Grayer novel."

I slapped my forehead and turned away from his and Kamryn's assessment of my behavior.

"Kamryn, is it?" Jordan asked in condescending fashion.

"Yes, and you are?"

"Taking my client to the VIP event readers paid a pretty penny to be part of." Jordan all but grabbed me by my elbow to drag me up the ramp beside the small stair case leading to the convention floor. I wrested my arm from his grip.

"Wait, dammit." I gestured Kamryn come with me. "There's food at parties. You need to eat."

"Did she pay?" Jordan snapped.

"She doesn't have to. She's my guest."

"That's not part of the contract," Jordan argued.

"Am I getting paid to do the event?"

"The publisher is. They have to recoup the money they've invested for you to be here. Since the damn books never arrived, this was plan B. You're only ten minutes late right now. We can still pretend you had a mishap with valet or something."

"I want her to come."

Jordan spun like turning on me, blood boiling beneath his rosacea. "Career ender, Tom! You've already disappointed them by being late. Don't break their hearts over a one night stand."

Kamryn gasped and cupped her hands to her chest. "Is that what this was?"

Jordan twisted to face her. "Duh. What did you think, honey? He has to leave at four AM. He has filming. A signing tour that takes him overseas. No time for a girlfriend. Men have needs. You fulfilled his. Thank you for your service."

"Jordan!" I couldn't believe the level of ... hell, what to call this disgusting display if inhumanity? "Kamryn, that's *not* what this was. I like you. A *lot*." *Could fall in love with you if this asshole wasn't in my life.* I glared at Jordan. "I do. Like her. A lot, Jordan. If you want to continue our professional relationship, don't ever talk to her that way again."

"That's cute and somewhat nauseating, Tom. We have a contract, and I don't recall kindness being one of your stipulations." He looked back at her. "Sorry, Miss Krause, he can't help it. He's a natural born actor."

I pushed Jordan aside, but he blocked my view of her turning her back on us. "Kamryn!"

She cast a last look at me. "He's right, Brogan. You're too busy. It's not my first rodeo. I know how show biz works."

With those final cryptic words, she turned her back and her door slammed behind her.

I pushed Jordan and barely restrained myself from punching him. After all, we had a contract, and I didn't want to make the news as the subject of his lawsuit. Not to mention, there were surveillance cameras watching us now.

"You told her your real name?" Jordan hissed. "What the fuck is wrong with you?"

I glared at him. "How did you know *hers*?"

"Didn't take a genius after the remark you made about her

to that reader who wouldn't shut the hell up and let you go. I just had to figure out which room she was booked under."

"No privacy. None. Never. I'm sick of this shit, Jordan. You just fucked up something good." I bent and held my knees, desperate to go to her room and beg her to open the door for me, to kidnap me and hold me hostage so this prick couldn't pluck my strings like a puppet master anymore. I needed to contact my lawyer as soon as I landed at the next location.

"Don't even think about it," Jordan said.

I scoffed and walked toward the ballroom, sent the sharpest glare I could as I stepped backward for a full view of his injured pride. "She's not a one-night-stand. I'm gonna fix it. All of this shit!" I turned my back on him and resumed my pissed pace.

"I didn't fuck it up!" he called after me. "I saved your life. You'll thank me one day."

I closed my eyes when I placed my hand on the door, paused for a beat. *She knows how show biz works... show biz. Elliot Meyers. What did she have on him and how did I stop her from making Jordan's dream of her permanent absence come true?*

"And here is the guest of honor now! Ladies and gents, Tom Snow reading as Detective Grayer!"

I smiled up at the emcee who'd caught my entrance, then waved to the crowd gathered to see me. A man like me didn't deserve their applause, and I was never more aware of my imposter syndrome than now, when I was celebrated as I knew with everything inside that I'd had a hand in breaking a heart who had a heart for others.

SOMETIMES, the only cure for what ailed was family, and though I seemed the last of my siblings to understand that, they'd all welcomed me with open arms. A week of recovery in the bedroom my brother and I once shared reminded me of my humanity, gave clarity on Jordan's behavior, proved beyond a reasonable doubt I needed to fire him. The how, when, why were the hard parts.

I played with my nieces and nephews, mowed my parents' lawn like old times, helped my brother at the family church. I may have impersonated him once or twice to peep on parishioners' confessions before he'd caught me and forced me into the other side of the box we used to play in when Dad was the head pastor.

"Something's eating you alive," Brylan said on the other side of the grate masking his features identical to my own. "We all know it, but everyone else is too polite for fear of scaring you away for another year."

"Twins know."

"Yeah, you've been dragging my mood for months now. I

can feel it no matter how far away you are. Please, for my sake, let it go."

I broke, confessed to feeling trapped by my success, to sitting on information I'd stolen from a woman I'd seduced.

"Information?"

"Yeah, Bry. It's bad. *Really* bad. Like un-alived bad. Everyone in the industry knows, but I stay away from what I don't want to know. I don't know what happened." My voice cracked, hands parted. "I can't explain why, but I care about this woman more than I want to. More than makes sense. I can't quit thinking about her, worrying about her, especially knowing what she knows. I don't know how she's functioning, how she's sleeping. She's caring for her mom who has Alzheimer's."

Brylan inhaled long and loud. "That's rough. We have a woman caring for her mother. The fire department says she keeps running away at night, that the mother is becoming physically abusive."

I winced. "That's awful. Like grandpa got with grandma before he went to the facility."

We sat in silence like we were both lost in our sad memories.

"Continue," he nudged. "You don't have to measure your words. Your secret isn't safe from God. He already knows."

"Okay, fine. We had the *best* sex, Bry. She's ... I dunno. I guess because I learned what she was dealing with, the connection was beyond physical. I seduced her, but she pulled my emotions into bed with her, too, and now I'm fu—screwed. What she's dealing with is hard enough, then I betrayed her trust and she has no idea, but I can't just sit on what I know without doing something."

"So, do something."

"It's not that easy. It could ..." I choked on the weight of guilt. "I don't want to make you a regular individual, if you know what I mean." He cleared his throat. I saw him pinch the bridge of his nose, though I couldn't actually see. Twin powers. "Bry, you the reason I've been feeling prodigal son vibes, dammit? You praying for me?"

"Of course. If you're gonna make me feel all this tension while I'm practicing piety, then I'm gonna force you to feel my conviction for you."

"I can't believe I'm saying this, but thank you. It's a great feeling knowing someone is praying when I feel so far from home."

"We're right here. He's always there, too."

My face fell into my hands. "I miss you. Miss this town. Miss that stupid little window dressing contest Mom used to win when she ran her craft store, the festivals for barely any reason, the parades, people who could care less about my fame and look at me like I'm nothing special. I miss ice skating on the lake and how we'd team up and play hockey with Ben and Barrett before they become too cool for us and left the nest for college and careers. You're blessed, man. I'm living a curse disguised as paradise."

"He's creative, Brogan."

I sniffled and pinched my nose to stymie tears. "You know it and I'm tired of dancing with him."

Brylan snorted to himself. "You remember when we volunteered to help run the sugar cookie contest tables? We put the wrong colored tops on all the icings and watched the carnage?"

We both laughed.

"Bry, you remember when we used to kidnap the Jesus statue from the altar and put it in front of houses we knew were doing stuff they shouldn't? We'd take those pictures and plant them at the police station, solve the crimes for the cops?"

"Easy to do when the crimes were so petty, they were committed by the guys we went to school with. Like who'd toilet-papered the coach's house, or who'd stolen the potted plants from Mrs. Jones's front porch."

I cringed. "Remember when we got the sheriff in trouble for sleeping with one of the deputies' wives?"

Brylan coughed. "Shh. Bro, no one knows it was us. Those old wounds live on to this day. Can you imagine the scandal if the new pastor of the church was outed as the guy who caused that rivalry?"

"Or the one who was responsible for the Jesus statue scandal?" I snickered. "You could just point the finger at me and say I was the one who did it."

"You were." He smiled. I felt his like mine. "I still have that old Polaroid we got at Hanson's Mercantile."

"Maybe we should kidnap Jesus and take Him and that camera for a spin. See what we can dig up."

"If that's the case, you want to take Jesus with you to the set of your show?"

"Ooh, burn!"

"Sorry, man. It slipped out."

"That's what she said."

"Brogan. You can't joke like that here."

"Brylan, Jesus knows we joke like this at home. Didn't you say there's no secrets from him?"

"Jesus knows, but that doesn't mean I want the parishioners to know."

"So we both hide things."

"We all hide things, Brogan. Not everyone needs to know everything. We are entitled to privacy and personal autonomy. It's when the things we hide hurt others that they become sin."

And now we'd come full circle back to what bothered me. I sat and stewed on the conviction I felt over hacking Kamryn's computer when she was showering. Sure, I'd done it to gauge her danger level, see if what she knew matched up to the things the industry knew.

"Life was easy when I didn't know what I was missing. Now, I look at you, all of your kids, your proximity to each other. I want a piece of it." Want Kamryn.

"You know, you don't have to take a piece, you can add one to the pie. It's more fun to give than take."

My head tilted back without a way to protect Kamryn, to help her, to be with her. "Ugh. Must you always be the voice of reason?"

"It's my job, my calling, Brogan. I'm not sure acting is yours for much longer." Brylan pushed a hand outside the curtain covering his side of the confessional and waved his fingers beyond mine. I smiled and grabbed his hand. "We're here. When you choose to join us. Come home. Be a nobody with the rest of us. Everyone's so used to seeing our face, they don't care about Detective Grayer."

"A prophet is never appreciated in his hometown."

"Thank God for that," he joked. "But no one would ever accuse you of being a prophet."

I squeezed his warm palm, then Dad reached inside the curtain and gripped both our hands. He didn't say anything, but part of me warred with shame in him hearing the things we'd talked of. He dropped our hands and left us alone. Brylan pushed out of his side of the confessional and pulled me into a hard hug. Sometimes, people needed hugs. Kamryn needed this. I had a hard time praying for myself, but for her, I found myself talking God's ear off.

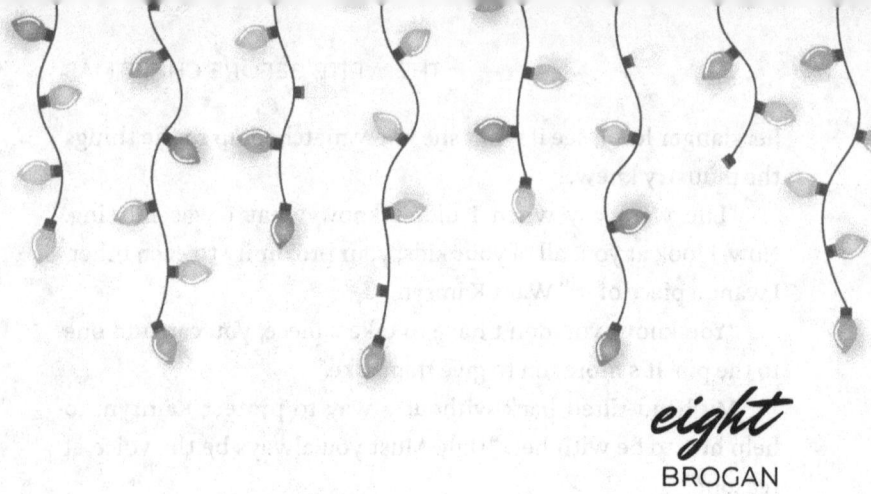

LIKE OLD TIMES, I sat on the porch and rocked my chair, watched the nature expanding in all directions. I'd always wanted to live in town, then town became a bigger town, until I called Sin City my humble abode. My roots were thirsting for the living water present in each of my family members and this land.

Mom took a rocking chair beside me and looked over the pasture. "Evelyn Krouse passed away right here in Evergreen Lake. Did you know she retired here? You went out into the world looking for love and she settled here. Ironic."

"That was childhood, Mom." I sent a desperate plea for her not to give me a hard time. "I didn't know of her passing or that she'd retired here." Was Kamryn here? Was that why I came home? Did her magnet pull me here? I took a deep breath. "She was part of our household for years even if she never knew it. The world lost a voice for truth."

She'd hummed her agreement, then allowed the silence I'd wanted to permeate the tension between us. I should've apologized for not calling, for missing Easter, but I chose distraction.

"Did I tell you I got to speak with her at the conference in Tahoe?"

You know, when I was only an hour from home and failed to stop by?

She'd gasped, chided me for failing to share, then asked how. I admitted I met her lookalike daughter, that she was pretty great.

"If you're friends, you should check on her. Pretty sure she lives in town."

"Yeah."

"You fire that horrible agent yet?" She poked at my weak spots.

I rocked a little faster. "Not yet. As horrible as he is, I can't find a place where he's breached his end of our contract. Believe me, I'm looking. After what he did at the convention—"

"Why put up with him? Breach the contract. Pay the legal fees. Buy your way out or something. You're making a ton."

"So is he. When you bring in the cash, leeches aren't easy to shake."

"What did I tell you about making a deal with the devil, Brogan?" Her chair rocked faster, her knuckles white on the arm rests. "I knew he'd come knocking and you opened the door and invited him in. Now, he's got you in shackles doing his bidding with those sex scenes in that show."

"For goodness' sake, Mom, there's only been three sex scenes and they're not that bad—"

"*Not that bad?* I haven't seen those parts of you since you were potty training, young man!"

"We didn't have actual sex and I hated every second of it! I can't stand her! Do you think I like being naked in front of like thirty people on set?"

"Don't you dare make me curse, Brogan!"

"Mom! I'm trying to tell you I'm sorry. That I know I'm in a bad place. That I want out because I met someone I can't quit thinking about and you're lecturing me about sex? You? Who has five living children and three miscarriages? Clearly you and Dad have tangled in positions like the one you're angry about quite a few times."

"Son, we're married and we didn't film it for the world to watch. We aren't making money selling it. Wait—did you just say you met someone?"

I groaned like Kamryn had when she'd been talking to her mom what felt a lifetime ago instead of just over a month ago. "Yes. Now I need—"

"Prayer? A miracle?"

"Yes," I sighed the answer, defeated, tired of fighting what my family had to offer.

Mom harrumphed, but jumped out of her chair and opened the screen door. "Beau! Come here!" She waved my father from the model car he was painting, then let the screen slam before she sat back beside me. "What's her name? So I can pray. For her."

I heard my eldest brother laughing as he came through the living room and pushed through the screen. "Wait. You telling me Bro has a crush on a girl?" Ben waited for me to stand then clapped his hand against my back after a tight hug. "Long time no see, man. You look good." He pulled his own rocking chair from the row and parked in front of us instead of single file. "Tell us about this girl. Is she real or a character from the show? Your co-star's hot. Something there?"

Mom snorted. "He says he hates her."

"Oh, me too." Ben crinkled his nose and switched to my team.

Brylan was next to let the screen door slam behind himself. He pulled his chair from its spot, said, "Spill it."

"Hey!" I protested. "I thought confession was sacred."

"Yeah, but I'm your brother. I thought you came to me as your twin, not your pastor. Tell them."

"Kamryn Krouse. She goes by Kamryn Kole—"

"Wait! Wait! Wait! Wait! Wait!" Brandy rushed through the screen and trotted to her chair beside Mom. "As in Kamrie's Korner? The bathroom blogger we followed for our road trips back in the day?"

"As in Evelyn Krouse's daughter?" Mom asked.

"This the one you said you seduced?" Brylan sold me out. "You were such a fan of that blog! You're a groupie but it's not for Evelyn. You slept with the blogger you used to follow, you dog."

"Guess you got me. I'm guilty of what fans have tried with me. I should be ashamed."

"But, you're not," Brandy added with a sly grin. "Thanks to her, I know what road trip bathrooms to avoid for diaper changes. She's a life saver. Wish she still ran that blog. I could use an updated list for the stations that have gone in over the last five years." She shook her head. "I can't believe it never dawned on me that Kamryn Kole was Kamryn Krouse of Kamrie's Korner. Her K's are as bad as the B's Mom cursed us with."

"I prefer blessed, thank you," Mom said.

"Mmhmm. Bet you didn't feel blessed when you were running through our names anytime one of us was in trouble. You called me all four of the boys' names when I was little."

Mom clucked her tongue. "And yet, you chose to carry the B Hive to a new generation."

Brandy huffed, though she wasn't annoyed. "Guess we're a family of hypocrites."

"Indeed," I agreed.

I heard the fridge slam. My niece hovered near the screen door like a spectator at the zoo animals on the other side.

"Brielle, did you ask if you could have that ice cream?" Brandy asked.

"Uncle Brogan bought it and said I could have as much as I wanted."

Brandy and Mom sent the same look my way before Brandy told her to eat it in the kitchen and keep it away from baby Bryce. "Better yet, I'm pressing pause." Brandy hopped up and stepped back out with her three-month old son. His feet kicked in footed pajamas. "Here, Uncle Brogan. Since you're such a good uncle you can spoil this one as well." I took the baby and tucked him into the crook of my arm. When he stared up at me, Brandy's hands gripped her hips. "Not fair. He doesn't rest like that for me."

"It's because you're food. He'll eat all the time. Boys are always hungry. Your brothers were just like him."

We gave a collective grossed out groan. Mom was happy to make us miserable.

"So," Brylan picked back up, "You seduced the daughter of that sweet old lady who used to report the news on the morning show before school?"

Ben held his hand like a stop sign. "Didn't you have a thing for her when you guys were like eight?"

"I'm gonna go join Brielle—"

"No!" Mom slapped Ben's thigh. Brandy slapped his arm, then, in unison with Mom, ordered me to, "Sit down, Brogan."

"This is the most I've seen Brogan in a year." Reprimand lit Brandy's eyes. "I heard Mom giving you the third degree on the sex scenes. I agree with her. I never wanted to see that side of you, but when I was at Sips on Main last month, I heard a lady ask Brylan's wife if you were identical in *every* way. I about lost my sh—*junk* when Sarah Beth didn't know how to answer."

"Dang!" I laughed and accidentally startled baby Bryce. I massaged one of his little feet and shushed him, then looked at Brylan. "Asking about the pastor's penis has got to be at least ten sin points straight off the bat! Add her to the prayer chain."

Mom shook her head. "What would your father say?"

He lazed through the screen door. "You're welcome for passing along good genetics." He winked at us and kissed Mom's gasp. Instead of taking his rocking chair beside Mom, he crossed his arms over his chest and leaned against one of the porch columns. "Brogan. Got yourself a girl. My advice, either write the sex out of the show and do right by her, or prepare to lose her forever, because she shouldn't have to share her husband with the world, or another woman."

"Whoa, whoa. Pop, I didn't say I was getting married—" I adjusted the baby while his eyes closed.

"You said you'd seduced her."

Ben lifted his bottle of beer and toasted me with a warm smile on his face. "You know your Word, Bro. Two bodies. One flesh." He took a satisfied drink.

Brylan nodded. "Hate to break it to you, but you're already married in the sight of the Lord."

This family enjoyed my squirming like a spectator sport.

"So, you banged the blogger who looks just like a younger Evelyn Krouse," Ben said. "Now, you think you're in love with her? How do you know? Did you grow a heart for Christmas in July? By the way, did you stop by the bank and see that huge wreath Dad and I built for the occasion?"

I shook my head.

"Speaking of!" Brandy interrupted. "Do you think you'll be here for the holidays? It's finally my turn to host Thanksgiving. Brandon and I bought our own house in January!" She squealed. "Guess who my next door neighbor was?"

"Who?" I'd searched their faces as they'd exchanged knowing smiles, albeit sad ones.

"Ms. Krouse and her daughter—Brielle! Stop! You're dripping everywhere!" Brandy sighed and apologized.

Ben shrugged and opened his legs to sink deeper into his chair. "Let her come outside. She can't ruin the grass."

"No," Dad said, "but she will attract ants."

"Exactly," Ben said. "She'll learn the way we did."

"He has a point," I agreed. Mom and Dad rushed to argue. The lot of us kids stared at their hypocrisy. "It was good enough for us, but you can't let it happen to her?"

"That's a grandchild," Mom said. "It's different."

Brandy told Brielle to stay in the kitchen again, then refocused on me. "I'm serious, Brogan. Ben lives an hour away but he makes time to come over several times a week. Barrett's on the oil rig, but he's coming."

"I don't know if I can get out of filming—"

"Please, bubba!" Brandy burst without composure. "You have to have a life! You can't live for these books and shows! They're not real! We are! Brielle loves you. Bryce is gonna love you. I can't let you break their hearts!"

The baby started crying. She reached for him, but I shifted him out of her reach like I used to with her dolls. "I'm not gonna break their hearts, Brandy. Damn." I ignored their chiding my language. "Does Kamryn live at that house or was she only there to care for her mother?"

Brandy said, "I haven't seen her since her mother passed, but there's been no for sale signs. There's also been no maintenance. The house is without power and the blinds are all drawn. I've thought of reaching out to her to see if she'd like any help clearing it out. Brandon has been mowing the yard so she doesn't get a notice from the city since we're right inside the historic district."

She started chatting about the decorations she had planned for Thanksgiving and Christmas, how they were blocked in during parades and festivals. She was far too delighted for someone preparing to be trapped in their home during those tourist booms.

"Okay," Mom said. "We know her name is Kamryn. That she needs prayers for—wait, do you know if she feels the same way about you?"

"I don't. We, uh, had—"

"Amazing sex," Brylan supplied, the little ass. "But, there was emotion. On his side."

Ben sucked his teeth before taking a long swig from his long neck. "You don't know if she was emotional? Isn't that all women are?"

Brandy punched his bicep. "He's right even if he's rude. Did you do something stupid?"

"No. But my agent was hella rude to her."

"Fire him," Dad said. "All in favor?"

"Say I!" Everyone said in unison.

"Have you talked to her?" Mom asked.

Baby Bryce gripped my finger while I caressed his tiny tummy. "I left her a note and she has my number."

"But she hasn't called or texted?" Brandy asked. "How long ago did you hook-up? Did she see the show and get upset?"

"Brandy, we slept together way after that. She's not a fan of mine, by the way. She doesn't watch the show or read my books."

"Good thing," Brylan muttered and stood from his chair. "I gotta get back home and change for Wednesday service." He leaned down and kissed the top of my head, then ruffled my hair to piss me off.

"Dick." My chair rocked when I shoved him.

"You always have the best parting lines, Bro."

Everyone said bye to him. The flock of hens meandered near

us. Mom reached into the sealed feed bucket and tossed a handful.

"Sacrifice," Dad said. "There's no greater love than to lay one's life down for a friend."

I huffed. "What do you mean, Pop?"

He didn't answer. He pushed away from the column and shooed the chickens away from the porch. Mom excused herself, said she'd be right back. "Wait, Beau!" She walked after him. "He asked what you meant. It's an open door, why don't you take it? You preach at him, but ask God to bring your prodigal back home. What more do you—" They rounded the side of the barn where we couldn't hear them argue.

Brandy sent me a sympathetic smile. "I can tell you. Brylan just taught on this not too long ago. He urged husbands to love their wives as Christ loved the church. Christ laid down his life for his friends. He called us friends. Get where I'm going?"

"You think I should quit the business?" I asked.

She bit her lip till it popped free from her teeth again.

Ben sighed and lowered his eyes to the concrete. "Bro, I'm not married, so I can't really speak from experience. You've made a lot of money, but if Brandy were the actress, in scenes like the one where she's pinned to the wall ... how do you think Brandon would feel?"

"He has a point, Bubba." Brandy moved into the closest rocking chair and grabbed my thigh. "If you weren't my brother, it would've been hawt, but reverse it and pretend it was Brandon with me at home, I'd want him to choose me and never kiss anyone else," she finished.

Ben looked over his shoulder like he sense'd Mom's wrath. "I'd better go. She doesn't look happy." He pushed up from his chair and handed me his bottle in exchange for stealing the sleeping baby. "Bye, bye little man," he made baby talk to Bryce, but aimed his words at me. I rolled my eyes, though I missed him.

"Love you, too, Ben."

He gave Bryce to Brandy, then clenched my shoulder, rocked my chair, held my eyes. "You're gonna do the right thing. I know it. You'll figure it out. I have faith in you."

My hand covered his. "Thanks, Ben."

He walked around the side of the house.

Brandy started tip toeing to the screen door. She lowered her voice to a whisper. "Guess who's passed out on the couch from her sugar high, Uncle Brogan?"

"You're welcome," I whispered back.

"I have to go feed him," she hissed under her breath and inched the screen open. "I love you, Bubba. Praying for both of you and all the things." Brandy darted inside just as Mom slid into back into her chair.

"So, sacrifice? Lay down my career?" I asked her.

"Brogan." She sighed my name like a curse. "You're a very generous person when you want to be. You laid down your life once for your friends and you scored your dream job reporting the news. You knew when you exposed the bad guys doing bad things to the kids in the productions that you could lose everything you hoped for, and you did it anyway. I was proud of that. We all were. You used the little power you had for good. That's called laying down your life for your friends. Sacrifice."

I CLOSED MY EYES, slapped my pencil onto a Steno pad, and massaged my pounding temples. Why did I have to choose an identity as an accountant? Just because I excelled at math didn't mean I wanted to make a career out of numbers. Just because I'd slept with Tom Snow didn't mean I cared about him. Couldn't quit thinking about him. Kept replaying what his agent said.

Weren't authors allowed to fire their agents? Was Brogan bound by something different between them?

I opened my desk drawer, pulled the scrap of envelope he'd torn and stuck to my hotel door. His handwriting was sloppy, but legible.

> Special K,
> I'd disappoint my whole family for you if I were allowed. Stay safe out there. Don't make me miss you forever.
> - B.S.
> PS - yes, those are my initials in case you

hadn't put that together on your own yet. Count it a blessing you never have to worry about those being your initials. K.S. sounds short for kiss and I like that. A lot.

How could I quit thinking of him when his damn show and face were everywhere? Had they always been everywhere and I'd just never noticed because I rarely had the chance to read or watch TV? Lord knew since Mom passed, I now had too much time. What had I always done with myself before I'd played nurse for her? The black monitor suspended from the ceiling in the corner called to me, tempted me to turn on Detective Grayer, to long for Brogan's face. What if he had another love scene? How would that make me feel watching him in passion with another? Even if he said he hated kissing his co-star ....

Poor Mom. She didn't understand why I'd cry when she watched her favorite show. When she forgot about her show, life was easier and harder at the same time. I'd turn on the *Price is Right* or *Murder She Wrote*. She'd not complain, but she'd also stopped walking, stopped eating on her own, then stopped eating for me altogether. The bittersweet blessing was that she'd never forgotten my name in the end. She'd also taken her final breath in my arms.

I sighed and tucked the note back in my desk, forced my attention back to the figures blurring in my distraction. This case was my obsession. I needed to lock in, to get my head back in the game so I didn't make Brogan miss me forever. As if I wasn't already doing that.

Pencil back in hand, I stared at the glowing computer monitor and wrote figures on the pad again, preferring analog to double check my work on the taxes I prepped. Admittedly, accounting paid me much better than journalism ever had.

Maybe I should give up doing what I loved and keep doing what paid the bills. The Elliot Meyers story was big enough to earn a fat paycheck. Or ... a pay off to keep me quiet.

"They make calculators for that."

My chair bucked against a row of filing cabinets at the sound of the unexpected voice. He gave a sheepish smile, thumb over his shoulder pointing to the door of my store front.

"You left it unlocked. Dangerous, considering it's after dark."

I pushed back from my desk and sidestepped him and the carrier at his feet, aimed for the lonely lobby. The glass door to my store locked under my thumb as I mentally braced for Josh's salt in my raw wounds. *What was my ex doing here?* He remained in the office.

"What brings you to my office, Josh? Need information on your new child tax credit?" I half-joked when I came back.

"I can't believe you're wearing those shoes to work." He ignored my joke. "Didn't you say you got them for me?"

I glanced at the high heels Brogan loved, too. "I got them for *myself* but wore them to surprise you when you came home from deployment. There's a difference."

"They're too risqué for the office."

My chin lifted. "I bought them to see where they take me. Maybe they'll help me hook someone who's also going my way." Too bad the man they'd hooked lost his grip on my line and swam away.

Perhaps they'd next hook the client who'd yet to take my planted recommendations and advertisements. If we didn't cross paths soon, I'd have to pass the information I'd thus acquired to someone with bigger chops and connections. Move on to another story altogether. Eating was important. So was not sleeping in your pretend office then hiding the evidence of your bed inside filing cabinets.

"Hooking is an apt phrase for those."

My eyes bugged. "You're being a dick. It's been a months, Josh. Aren't you over it by now?" If I didn't know any better, maybe he cared more for me than he'd thought if his jealousy said anything. Too bad I wasn't watching Detective Grayer so I could point the remote up to the screen and tell him I'd hooked that man. "*I* didn't sleep with anyone else while you were gone. If anyone gets to be mad, it's me. Clearly, I wasn't enough to satisfy you."

"Stop. Let's not make this worse. I came to apologize." He grabbed my hand and coaxed me into his embrace. Before Brogan, this may have broken me. Now, I only wished for strong arms around me while firm hands kneaded the knots of tension from my back. Josh couldn't hold a candle to Brogan. "I'm sorry." Josh broke my thoughts. "The shoes are sexy as hell. The bikini was, too. You're mad at me and I hate it."

I rolled my eyes and pulled away, then knelt before the little car seat. "Let's see if you're any good at this baby-making thing." I lifted the pink blanket. Underneath rested a head of fine black curls, puckered lips motioning in a sleepy suckle, eyelashes lying over rosy, chunky cheeks. Okay, so maybe my ovaries clenched a little.

When I looked up, Josh's smile radiated a soft pride I'd never seen before. "Surprise, I have a little girl to punish me for all the women I've hurt, including you. This one pulls my finger like a club, and I follow her command like a cave man."

"She's beautiful, Josh."

"Thank you. So are you. I'm so sorry, Kamryn. You were my friend before we ever hooked up. I shouldn't have treated you that way. Last year, I didn't tell you about my itch to sleep with someone because I was itching to sleep with you and hadn't gained the courage yet, especially since we'd been roomies under the circum—"

My hand waved between us. "All water under the bridge now, but I appreciate the sentiment. If we were meant to be, we'd be. I miss your company, but the distance has cleared the accidental hearts from my eyes."

He caught my hand. "I'm sorry about your mom. I want—"

"Josh, I forgive you. I'm not in love with you. I'm still convinced love is a non-existent product sold in programming to keep us unfulfilled and unsatisfied." *If only.* I wriggled my hand free and wiped my sweaty palm on my skirt. "You were the first guy in a while to make me question being single, that's all. Easy to inflate a little crush into something way more when it was just the two of us living together. I'm glad you've found a woman who'll love you for life."

"Oh, she was a one-night stand. We're getting to know one another, but—"

"Josh, I meant your daughter. Relax. This will all work out."

The tension in his frame eased. "Thank you, Kamryn. I've never felt this way before. We haven't taken her in public yet. You were the first person I wanted to show her off to. You know, after my parents."

Was he that dense? Did he not realize how insensitive he was? Rather than give him a lesson on thinking beyond his own wants, I said, "I bet they're thrilled."

"Totally. My mom lost all hope I'd ever give her grand babies, then I surprised her. It was epic. I got this big box, no lid, just the appearance—" We turned at the small rap on the glass door. Josh's brow furrowed. "Don't open it."

My stomach jumped. I didn't recognize the face, however I *did* know the calling card. *Had the bait finally worked? Who else but a criminal would seek an accountant after hours?*

Suddenly, I needed Josh and his little cherubim out of sight, out of danger if this was whom I suspected.

I cleared my throat and any anxiety he may have spied.

"He's a client who arranges to come in at this time because he works long hours," I lied. "He usually makes an appointment."

"No appointment tonight? Don't you think that's a little hinky?" Josh asked like a person with common sense should.

"Hinky?" I chuckled. "Who uses that word outside a mystery novel? He's safe, Josh."

Josh scoffed. "Bullshit. He why you wore those shoes to work?"

"He's why I'm politely asking you to leave my office so your daughter will have a chance for siblings." I kissed his cheek and lifted her carrier. He followed me outside the private office into the lobby.

"He doesn't require a late appointment for nothing," Josh persisted. "I don't feel good about it. How long has this been going on?"

"Since before you and me slipped up and started sleeping together." *Well, at least my investigation into Mr. Meyers, so not a total lie.* "Don't worry, Josh. I'm not his type."

Josh had natural instincts, rarely reacted to other men around me, so when his alarm bells rang, mine chimed, too. If I had any shot at keeping character, I couldn't let him deter me from my goal. Besides, he didn't know to call me by the pseudonym I'd created. He'd wreck my work before I could pull the fish from the water.

I unlocked the door with my keys. The well-dress stranger greeted us and held the door open for Josh to lug the baby seat across the threshold. Josh thanked him for his hospitality but eyed him same as he'd probably eye future men barking up his daughter's tree.

"Good evening," I said. "Feel free to settle into the office. I'll be just a couple minutes."

"Very well." He obediently disappeared behind my office door and I knew I was right about this one. No one else had shown up after hours the entire time the sign was on the door.

"You *are* his type," Josh hissed under his breath. "He checked out your shoes. Twice."

"Don't worry, Josh. I'm just a boring accountant and now you're just another dad." My eyes flared that he not blow my cover. His narrowed like he contemplated doing just that. I dropped the flare for a silent plea and another hug.

He squeezed me harder, told me to call if I needed an ass kicked. "I might be just another dad, but there's a super power in that that I didn't have before. I'm not afraid to use it on bad guys here in the states, ya hear?" I'd miss his strength and protection. I couldn't say he had what Mom dubbed husband hands, but he did make a woman want them all over her again and again. Was that why I'd thought I'd fallen for him? Brogan effed that up for me, too. There'd never be another massage during sex, I could almost guarantee that. Even if there was, there was no one else with hands like his.

Don't make me miss you forever.

Welp, you sonuvabitch, you make me miss you everyday, so I hope you're missing me this very second!

I pulled away from what I knew would be our final embrace, and closed the door. Josh stared while I locked the bolt with my key. In case the stranger was watching, I turned off the lights in the lobby to steal his view of Josh's concern.

Why did Josh suddenly care so much? Why did men seem to only want what they couldn't have?

"Hope I didn't intrude on anything," my client said when I returned to my office. "Is that your baby?"

"No, I'm not the mother. That's my friend, Mr...?"

"Mr. Black." He offered his hand.

"Nice to make your acquaintance." We shook, then I tucked myself behind my desk and pulled myself close to the surface, though I clenched my hands in my lap beneath to disperse the tension in my body.

He chuckled to himself. "Your friend is protective."

"I told him he has nothing to worry about. You're not about to make a liar?"

He laughed again. "No. But my boss has an emergency. Somehow his personal investments crossed ties to his charities and he needs to separate his assets." *Was he onto wife number five's plan to divorce?* "Something isn't adding up. I'm not sure who made the error, but he's in the red. This can't happen before the end of the fiscal year and especially before the holidays. We don't want to lose tax exemption status."

Indeed, something's not adding up ... Why would they if the classification was correctly filed ...?

"Charities?" I pretended I didn't know.

He handed me a portfolio and at least four hours of preliminary work. "I'll wait in the parking lot."

My chair rocked under my sudden shift. "You want this done *tonight?*" I gaped. "There's no way." After all, I'd just had a full day of playing games on my phone, cruising social media for potential projects, filling my Pinterest board, doing taxes for the stylist next door for the sake of appearances ....

"He needs this done *now*. It's urgent." Nothing in his flat expression changed.

I flipped the manilla folder open for my first true peek behind the curtain, retained a professional annoyance to hide my giddiness. At the sight of Elliot Meyers' name along with the titles of at least three shell companies, butterflies of excitement fluttered above the pit of dread in my belly.

"There's another month before filing starts." I combed through tax files. "These accounts show quarterly payments. If there's an error, I'll need fresh eyes to find them." My weary eyes met his. The stern set in his jaw wasn't promising. I sat back and folded my hands on the desk. "To your knowledge, did Mr. Meyers forget to turn in a set of figures?"

"He wasn't specific. The discrepancy was found this afternoon. He's lost trust in his accountant." *Would that be his wife? Or, a current mistress perhaps?* "He'd like a fresh set of eyes who has no stake in the game. He'll pay whatever you want. Please."

"Should I be concerned?" I asked, tension cooling my limbs like ice. *Sure, now the survival instinct kicks in?*

"No," Mr. Black said. "His annual vacation is coming up. He'd rather not worry about anything."

Or the appearance of tax evasion? Using his darling charities and shell corporations to launder money to fund special interests groups?

My hands unfolded as I stood from my chair. I squared my shoulders. "I want to meet him."

"He will not allow it."

"I'll accept nothing less than face-to-face business dealings. I've worked for years to establish my business and reputation. I'm not taking the fall for an error purposely kept from me. If you've found me, it's because word's gotten around that I'm discreet and I'm good, but I'm also well-paid and protected for my services. Knowing my client face-to-face is part of the protected assurance I'm not being pulled into a crime."

Damn, I hope that didn't sound as clumsy as I felt trying to justify my motive.

"That's impossible. He may be able to make one meeting but not every one of them."

"Tell you what. I will audit these files for discrepancies, then I'll have them sent to his office with a bill for my services, but I do not agree to any further services under the terms you're offering."

Mr. Black lifted his buzzing phone to his ear. His eyes held mine while I wondered if Josh was still in the parking lot waiting for Mr. Black to leave me alone. He replaced the phone inside his pocket.

"Mr. Meyers has agreed to your terms if you do him this favor."

How did Mr. Meyers know my terms, my issues with his dealings, any of my concerns without Mr. Black uttering a word other than yes, sir on the phone? If he was willing to record our conversations, or put them on secret speaker phone or bluetooth, whatever, he had time to meet. Creepy.

"Please, Ms. Hughes." My alias. "*Please*. He needs someone he can trust."

Fear lanced my veins. If *I* was his last best hope, that meant the ones who'd gone before me may be on the run or dead for knowing too much.

"Right. That's why he's cool listening on a recorded line, but can't show his face?" I smirked.

"The file is yours for the night. Mr. Meyers agreed to your terms. I'll be in the parking lot."

Mr. Black waited for no arguments. He stood and exited the building.

I locked the door behind him, though I wanted to shove a desk in front of the entrance. If Mr. Black was his protective detail, this tiny lock was merely a nuisance.

Back at my desk, I collapsed into my chair and rolled against the filing cabinets. A long sigh pushed through my nostrils. My knee bounced. Intuition was a bitch. While others were prepping for Christmas festivities, I was afraid I'd just invited a host of demons into my life. Careful what you wish for ....

Rather than sit and allow fear to screw everything I'd worked for, I grabbed an EMF meter and closed my office door. For the next twenty minutes, I swept the entire office until I found the tiny bug I'd suspected.

Ironically, the listening device looked like a tiny bug

perched on the underside of the leaves on the potted money tree decorating the corner of my office.

I grinned and sat back at my desk, muttered a few natural frustrations with Mr. Meyers and Mr. Black. My white manicure hovered over my silenced photo app as I snapped images of the documents. I opened my texts and prepped to send them to my private investigator.

> Finally found the right bait bc the shark took my hook!

My lip pinched under my teeth. Aaron wasn't my contact anymore. His gifts were the parting sort. Sure, he'd thrive on this proof that he'd been right about the danger, but these would also put him and his family at risk.

Dammit. I deleted the text and replaced the burner phone he'd supplied before wishing me well.

I pulled out my real phone and silenced the photo app, repeated my actions.

I'd not texted Brogan once. He'd also not texted me. The handwritten letter was special because it was personal, his handwriting, the oils from his fingers, probably the saliva from his tongue to stick the envelope to the door. In my head, texting him seemed too impersonal and ruined the beauty of his parting words in the note. Like they bandaged the wounds his asshole agent gouged into my heart.

But ... Brogan was also the only other person who knew my plight, knew the danger, possibly some I wasn't yet aware of ....

If this story killed me, Brogan might be brave enough to publish it in my honor, bring justice to my murder ....

Despite my every rule against what I was about to do, I sent the images to him.

> Not a smoking gun by itself, but added to what I already have, it could bring a conviction in court

I didn't expect him to reply right away, but to my surprise, he did.

> 😷 holy shit
>
> Special K! 🎉🎉🎉
>
> She speaks, lives, breathes! 🖤
>
> Hallelujah! 🙏

A huge smile split my grief in half. Thrills filled my belly and tingled to the tips of my prancing fingers glancing the screen of my smart phone.

> Ah, finally proof of life outside of TV and magazine pictures! 🙄
>
> Thought your agent may have deleted my number to keep Romeo from Juliet

> He's unhinged 👀

> 😆 true story
>
> You should've seen him on the flight outta there. My dad wasn't as pissed when he caught me in the backseat of his car with the deacon's daughter. Smh.
>
> I wanted to text you, call you, everything with you for months, but the general consensus on advice from readers was to give you space, let you reach out when/if you're ready 😬

> AWWWW!! 🥺 You talked to readers about me?

> On the down low. After your mom passed. It was so hard not to reach out to you. To track you down and stand beside you for her funeral. I'm so so sorry, Kamrie 🤍

Tears filled my eyes like Mom was over my shoulder giving her little thump like I'd better jump rather than stand and think of the fear.

> I didn't have a funeral. She donated her body to science. I get her ashes in the mail in about a year. When I have her memorial, I'll put in a request you be by my side.

> I'll be there

> Pinky promise?

> pinky promise 🤍

> What's your email?

> BSpays@writingBS

> Why?

> Nice email addy 😊

> Thanks 😎 Can you tell I'm out of love with my career? Feel the bitterness in the air?

> Is that the chill? 😬

> I thought it was because Christmas is around the corner. Silly me.

> Can I call?

If I removed the bug from the plant, they'd know I'd found it. I couldn't call him without them listening. Dammit. I was so relieved to hear from him. To not have this awful thing hanging between us. To know he missed me. That I wasn't alone in my misery of missing him.

> I wish. I can't exactly have phone conversations right now…

Is that asshole with you?

Don't let him touch you, Kamryn!

He's not in the business of pleasure

He's a mean guy

Plays the perfect Santa for those charity events

Unleashes like a psychopath trapped in a padded room against his will when he takes off the costume

Don't ask how I know

Just trust me

> Okay, okay! 😥

> Calm down with the rapid fire texts!

> He's not with me and I won't let him touch me

> Chill it down

I will NOT chill 😾

I've stayed chill for months worrying, waiting, wishing for any sign that you're okay

I miss you more than I want to

I'm miserable

I want to go home

…and take you with me… 🙁

> That sounds wonderful

97

I miss you, too

Please, don't let him do anything...

Why do you think I wanted your email?

I'm protecting myself

If something happens to me, you're the only one I trust to hit publish and tell the world

Don't argue

Just do what you used to if it comes to that

The shark just bit my line

I'm reeling

His texts paused while I encrypted the email and attached every zipfile I had on Elliot Meyers. After a while, his name flashed on my notifications. I swiped the phone and glanced at my office door, the feeble lock between me and Elliot's goon, Mr. Black.

What's ur email so I'll know 2 check

KamriesKorner@blogger

It's my old email from my teens

Gotcha

I thought he might open the files and remark about my attention to detail, add tidbits like critique, but nothing else came, so I locked my personal phone back inside a hidden desk drawer. This way I wasn't desperately checking every notification to light my screen.

Over the next several hours, I poured through records I'd

never seen before, accounting for investments and purchases, exemptions claims, a litany of legal loopholes, but nothing gaming the system. Was the game on me? I thought of Brogan's messages and prayed not.

ten

KAMRIE

"HMM-HMM-HMM." A throat cleared.

"Ugh. Lori, it's Saturday! Lemme sleep and I'll quiz you for math later."

"Hmm-*hmm*!"

I whined and fluffed my pillow but punched solid wood.

My eyes bugged open while my knuckles splintered in pain. I rubbed my aching hand and jerked upright. My bleary gaze took in the paperwork spread over my desk, who the pages belonged to, what my job was.

Shit!

"Cassandra Hughes?" A tall figure in front of me took shape through the fuzz in my eyes.

Was this real? Maybe I was still in a dream?

"Yes." I nodded, blinked for clarity. "Sorry, I'm confused. Who are you and how did you get inside my office?"

"You have ink on your cheek." He rubbed his like a mirror. When I didn't move a muscle, he cleared his throat again. "Elliot Meyers. You wanted to see me?"

In a flash, my vision and objective cleared. The chair groaned as I kicked the leather from under my bottom and stood awkwardly in last night's high heels. "Mr. Meyers! Finally. I'm so sorry to be meeting you for the first time this way." I walked around my desk, wobbly for a beat, hand extended. He took my hand in his right, but cupped his left hand over the top, held eye contact.

"The pleasure is mine." I caught his eyes on my shoes before his gaze returned to my face. "I'm glad to make your acquaintance. You've been instrumental in my success."

"Excuse me?" My brow furrowed.

He gave a meek smile. "I have a confession to make. I test everyone I work with under an alias beforehand to confirm quality. Sips and Suds car wash?"

My eyes widened while my smile erupted. "Okay, I *loved* that account, but I admit I felt I was being trolled. After all, the name implies drinking then driving."

A wry smile stole the timid one and I had a very hard time equating the power broker in pictures and videos, not to mention Brogan's warnings, with the demur man before me.

"Yes, but we do—"

"Mocktails," we said in unison.

"I went and got my mocktail," I admitted. "A little out of the way, but it was a very pleasant time out while getting my van detailed. You're likely popular with suburban housewives."

I earned a hearty laugh. "You might be right. I'm glad you enjoyed it." He released my hand. "Forgive my messenger for scaring you last night. Neither of us were trying to be evasive. I'm a very busy man, as I'm sure you inferred from my finances."

I didn't want to appear I'd inferred too much from his financial records, so I simply nodded. "Thank you for taking time from your busy schedule to meet with me. While you're here, would you mind taking a look at my work, this way we're on the same page?"

"Happy to. I've cleared my schedule. We are free to crunch numbers. That is, if they're still visible on the page. We may need to turn your cheek toward the light for a portion of those figures." He grinned while I cupped my cheek.

"Oh, gosh, I'm sorry." My face lit on fire with embarrassment. "I've never fallen asleep on the job before. I'm positive I finished everything before passing out. I'd rather double check, though."

"I'd rather you double check also, Miss Hughes? Mrs. Hughes?" He angled his head, eyes inspecting my hands.

"Miss. I'm not married. Or dating. Well, I'm not in a relationship. I date."

His lips twitched. "Miss Hughes, should I be seated?"

"Oh, sorry. Yes, of course." I gestured toward the same chair Mr. Black had taken the night before. Though I wanted to pry about his personal assistant, as well as call his shit about bugging my office, my intuition urged me to play dumb. After all, an accountant wouldn't readily own electromagnetic frequency detection devices. Unless they hunted ghosts in their spare time, that is.

"Your feet must be killing you if you slept in your high heels."

I looked down at my feet. They did hurt pretty bad now that the fatigue cleared my senses.

"I've a proposition for you," Mr. Meyers said. *Did I want to hear any propositions from this man?* "Gather these files. I'll take them to my place while you go home and change into something more suited to teaching me math for a day. You did say you'd quiz someone named Lori, and I could use a nice refresher before you lay into me about my F in accounting."

"Lori?" I asked, confused.

He had the courtesy to look embarrassed, for me. Not

himself. "You were talking in your sleep. You told someone named Lori you'd quiz her in math if she'd let you sleep."

My brow cocked. "Wow. Gotta love dreams. I don't even know a Lori," I lied.

"You can't tell me you don't quiz math, because you're a genius to do this job."

"Mr. Meyers. You do get an F for failing to turn in all your work, but I think we should continue while I'm in pain as it will propel me to take less of your time."

"An F for failing to turn in all of my work, eh?" He sat back and smirked like he was impressed I'd caught on to his game. Another test. Fabulous.

He confessed, then said, "I can't focus knowing you're in pain because of me. It's my fault you worked all night."

"On a fake set of documents, I presume? You made me work all night after I'd told Mr. Black I was exhausted."

"I'm not sorry. You proved your tenacity and attention to detail even under exhaustion. Mr. Black has brought to attention how I've devoted my time to lesser important matters, but that boring numbers are what keep my fortunes flowing so I can keep the fun going. That means *we* need to spend more time together." He gestured between us and I saw my first true glimpse of the player who made women feel safe enough to drop their guards against him.

I fought the urge to roll my eyes. "I appreciate that." My hands rushed to stop his from lifting the paperwork. "What are you doing?"

"Gathering the files so you may change into something more comfortable. Let's regroup at my penthouse."

"I can't allow you to have these until I've signed off on them. You can claim they're fake, but they are real. It's like reading a book with missing chapters. You've admitted to tricking me twice for your personal satisfaction, so no offense, but I'm not going to your penthouse. I don't trust you."

The player dropped his game while I gave the face that made me a fantastic poker player.

"I didn't see it that way, but I suddenly understand why you do. Please forgive me? My home office contains all of my files. You'd be free to immerse yourself in anything and everything you find until you're content I'm not hiding anything from you. Whatever it takes to earn your trust and prove I'm an honest man who's been taken advantage of so many times in the past, I have trust issues myself. Why else would I have tested your ability?"

Because liars detect other liars.

Mr. Meyers pushed his glasses up his nose and shifted under my scrutiny. *Why hide my annoyance?* An accountant would've felt affronted. Disrespected.

I walked him back into the lobby, realized he'd not only unlocked my business door, but my office door to invade my privacy.

"Oh, dear. I forgot to lock the door." I feigned alarm I truly didn't have to fake.

"You locked it," he said, "but when you didn't answer your phones or the knocks on the door, I had Mr. Black pick the locks so I could check on your safety. Again, please forgive me."

I blinked hard, stared, unable to form proper words for such an improper situation. He held my stare. Finally, I said, "Which penthouse? The one in Los Angeles, New York, or Las Vegas? I'll need transportation allowance, per diem for meals, mileage."

His head ticked to the side. "You drive a hard bargain. And, if you didn't know me, how did you know about my penthouses?"

I remained neutral. "I didn't know you, however, once I saw

the names of the charities, I did my research, then did a little digging on you to satisfy my personal curiosity."

"Oh, and what did you find?" Mr. Meyers studied me like a new set of expensive golf clubs he wanted to get on the green as soon as possible.

I pretended not to notice. "You're about to be divorced for infidelity."

He play winced, rocked on the balls of his feet while stuffing his hands in his pockets. "You're not one for BS."

Depends on the type, hehe.

"I like that," he added. "Let's do Vegas. I keep my files in a safe there. You can work, then maybe we can play?"

I shook my head. "I don't play with married men, and I'm also a professional, Mr. Meyers. I'd never date a client."

"I'd never ask you to, Miss Hughes. Go home. Pack. Meet me on the tarmac at this address tomorrow morning."

He handed me a business card with a handwritten address on the back, then walked outside. Mr. Black opened the back door of a black SUV. Elliot Meyers got in. I watched the pair drive out of the parking lot and wondered what I'd just gotten myself into.

I walked back into my office and opened the desk, then unlocked the hidden drawer.

FYI I'm headed to Vegas

Perfect 🔥

What an odd response. No five why's?
No when? Where? How?

You okay?

Mhm

Bizzy on set

Grayer films n Vegas

Agent up ass

Txt when u arv

My eyes narrowed when he didn't reciprocate my pinky promise. Something wasn't right, but I didn't have time to dally. I had a case to crack and criminals didn't wait nor sleep on their sinister plans.

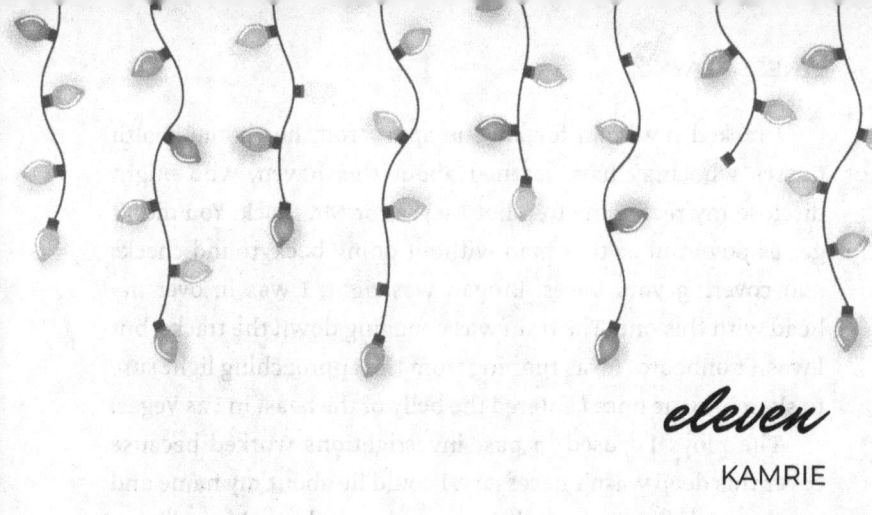

GO HOME AND PACK A BAG. *Meet me at the tarmac in the morning.*

I peeked between the slats of the wooden blinds. Every time dogs from the nearby pet rescue barked in a chorus, I worried he'd sent me home to have Mr. Black follow, that he'd discover my true identity.

I let the slat fall back into place, tugged the blackout drapes across the windows as twilight traded the merry daytime activities for scores of Christmas lights. The sounds of pedestrians heading for festivities had me on edge, their voices turning automatically to Elliot Meyers' barking orders to Mr. Black in my imagination.

Paranoid, I paced the house, haunted also by the mess I'd left when I'd fled Mom's passing in this place. She was everywhere. I couldn't be here anymore. I'd never intended to stay beyond caring for Mom anyway.

Had I ever publicly told anyone about Mom's place in Evergreen Lake?

That was her point in buying this old house, wasn't it? Privacy? Refuge from her celebrity?

I racked my brain for anyone apart from her home health nurses who may have learned about this haven, who might disclose my real name to Elliot Meyers or Mr. Black. You didn't get as powerful as that man without doing background checks and covering your bases. Brogan was right; I was in over my head with this one. The train was chugging down the tracks, but I wasn't onboard. I was running from the approaching light sure to slam into me once I entered the belly of the beast in Las Vegas.

The ploys I'd used in past investigations worked because cover this deep wasn't necessary. I could lie about my name and background, flirt my way into a man's mind, get him talking, the information flowed, then I'd do the write up and be out of the area in no time, no one the wiser.

This case was a career maker or career breaker.

Or, should I say, career-ender?

The idea that Brogan's agent viewed me in the same light as I viewed the weighty consequences if this investigation went bad made me sick. Imagining that horrible man having Brogan's ear, knowing he was manipulating Brogan into thinking I was poison, how could I contend?

I chuffed in bitterness. If I wanted to protect Brogan, I should've kept my information close to my chest. Now he had access to the files I shared, knew the toxic murderer manipulating me while I'd planned to manipulate him. Was I so naïve to think Elliot would, at my behest, bring his documents to my fake store front? That I'd catch him in my hidden cameras with the files in hand? Release the video proof and take the credit for a major win in the war on crime?

"Stupid, Kamryn! Stupid, stupid, stupid!"

I yanked my suitcase from the closet and rifled through the clothing I'd never unpacked after Brogan and I slept together. My fingers traced the undershirt he'd accidentally forgotten, or had he purposely left that with me because he somehow knew I'd pull his scent to my nose and miss him?

The clothing I kept at the store front was too formal. I wasn't going on this trip in high heels and a pencil skirt. I'd hooked the shark. I didn't want him to want to eat me.

I threw sweats and graphic tees inside with socks and granny panties no woman liked admitting she owned. If Elliot tried anything with me maybe he'd take one look at those and turn up his nose.

I never should've agreed to his terms. If only I'd said I didn't feel comfortable entering his private domain. No. I had to go and show off that I knew too much about him the way he'd challenged my alias's abilities. Pride goes before the fall. Accepting the invitation to his penthouse placed me in his realm, on his turf, and killers liked herding their prey to their hunting grounds to have the upper hand.

I paused at the sound of boisterous laughter and longed to join them, to visit the few acquaintances I'd made when I'd push Mom in her wheelchair to the town square during her final spring and summer. Those pleasant forays to Sips on Main, the local library, shopping at Hanson's Mercantile, my weekly staycation at Read Between the Wines when caring for Mom only meant making meals and helping her tidy the house. She'd deteriorated rapidly after I'd left to attend the convention. The nurses told me changes could do that.

"She wanted you to go, and you did what she wanted, there's nothing wrong with that. But, she was used to you being here with her, had her routine. When we come in, we aren't you. We can't replicate everything you do. The confusion is almost too much for her brain to cope with. Prepare yourself for sharp dives."

All of the serenity and simplicity of her merely needing my

helping hands turned to rushes into the police station when Mom started sneaking out of the house.

"Hey, hey, hey. Kamrie, relax. She's okay," a fire fighter assured after his cherries flashing through my window woke me in the middle of the night. He'd met me in the driveway where he'd braced her back and held her hand as she'd shuffled in a daze toward the front door.

"Dear, Lord, how is she okay?" My voice cracked. "It's not okay. I put bells on all the doors after last time. How did she get out? Will I be fined?"

He'd said, "No fines, but I'm being transferred to Lake Tahoe next week. If Chief catches her instead of me, he'll have no choice." He'd helped her into the living room. The bells piled in the corner behind the door. I gaped at the impossibility of how quiet she'd had to be to accomplish her escape! Not only had she removed the bells from the front door, but every damn door in the house! She couldn't even walk in a straight line or hold a cup without a tremor in her hands! Was she faking?

My eyes had drifted toward him noticing the piled bells, too.

"Look, Miss Kole. You didn't hear this from me, but either you put her into a home for her own good or lock her in her bedroom at night. You know, like you'd put a toddler in a crib to keep them safe from themselves?"

"How am I supposed to do that? I'm not putting her into a home when I'm perfectly capable of doing what the nurses do, and I'm here around the clock."

We'd watched Mom hobble into the kitchen for a cup of water.

He lowered his voice and tapped the doorknob. "Turn the knob around so it locks from the outside."

I'd gaped like he was insane. "I could never do something so barbaric."

"It's not barbaric. It's for her own good so she doesn't get hit by a car or something. Pastor Brylan at the old church in the square knows a place that won't cost a fortune if you can't bring yourself to keep her safe from herself and others."

"Isn't that abusive?"

"Is it abusive to put a toddler in a play pen to keep him from walking into the street when you want to sit outside and enjoy life?" He'd looked beyond me, nodded toward the kitchen. "Might want to put some baby proof covers over the gas knobs on the stove, too. Don't want to blow yourselves up when you turn on a light or use the fireplace."

Mom fumbled with the knobs. I'd run to stop her, but she grabbed the tea kettle and took a swing. I took the hit with my forearm instead of my face, then yanked it from her hands and caught the slap aimed for my face mid-strike.

"No, ma'am!"

Her face ripened red with rage. "You don't tell me what to do. I'm an adult! This is *my* house."

I'd closed my eyes and willed myself to be patient with her. By the time I'd turned to thank the fireman, he and his truck were gone.

In the here and now, I looked down at the backwards doorknob to her master bedroom. The little childproof cover still encased the side she'd tried to turn so many times.

You're free now, Kamryn. Your time was served. You did right by her. The absolute best you could. You couldn't do any better.

So why did I ache like I could've done more?

Was this how troops felt when returning from war?

Everyone expected life to go on when on the outside things looked the same, but on the inside, everything changed. Mom's illness seemed to steal ten good years of the youth I had left. All the gritty investigations, the dirt and misdeeds I'd uncovered, never sapped me the way this journey had.

I looked through the slats again, considered the church who'd provided meals when I'd never attended a single service. The woman next door with the perfect little family put Mom and me on a prayer chain. Funny. Never did I step foot inside that building, but I'd admired the beauty of the stained glass and steeple numerous times. Now that I was afraid to step foot outside Mom's house the church seemed safer than this place. Did churches still provide sanctuary to those in peril?

I could force myself to finish packing Mom's things, take them for donation to thank them for their kindness, ask for refuge if Elliot came out of the crowds enjoying their cookie contest.

Before I talked myself out of a moment of courage, I grabbed the childproof knob cover and snapped it off, then opened the door to Mom's room.

Her perfume mixed with the lingering stench of stale urine. Didn't seem to matter how many times I'd washed her sheets, I couldn't get rid of that ammonia.

At once, I charged inside and balled those sheets into a contractor bag. Time to quit hiding from the hard shit. Mom never hid from it, nor did she shelter me. She'd raised me to be brave even in the face of emotion.

My arms shoved inside the first coat I found in Mom's closet; a pink tweed trench number. I tied the bag and hoisted it the way Elliot always did the Santa sacks of gifts for photo ops. Had he ever carried bodies in those bags?

I wrestled the nasty bedding on my back and managed to open the front door.

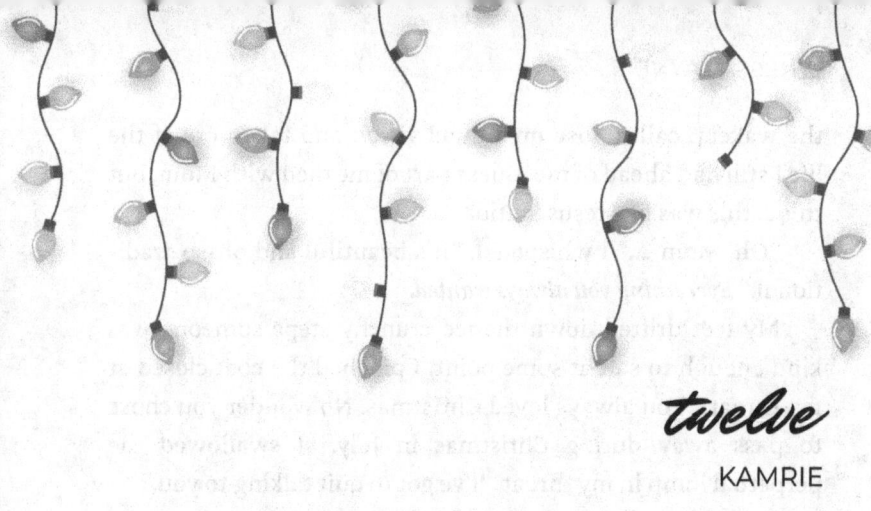

twelve

KAMRIE

WHEN I STEPPED onto the front stoop, the view ceased my cloudy breath, and I understood why Mom fell in love with this place. The bag dropped from my back and slapped the concrete beside my feet. While I was living inside a fake store front during the longest fishing expedition in history, the town transformed into a winter wonderland I hadn't quite noticed during the drive home in the daylight.

Christmas lights flickered and blazed bright like beacons of hope, each yard and home more like a child's fantasy of ginger-bread houses so quaint Santa might leave the North Pole for. Even my own yard outlined in a tidy row of colored lights. How did I miss those earlier?

The grass was crisp and clean, even if dead, which meant someone mowed my lawn in my absence before the seasons changed. Wow. I hadn't thought to hire someone for that. I was a bad neighbor. Somewhere I had a wonderful neighbor I'd like to thank. I felt bad for not knowing anyone I'd lived closest to for the better part of a year. The hazards of writing were becoming a hermit, but this was a little embarrassing and quite the wakeup call to lose my tunnel vision and take note of the life I still had ahead of me. Guess part of me died with Mom, but this ... this was like resuscitation.

"Oh, Mom ...." I whispered. "It's beautiful and oh-so-traditional." *Everything you always wanted.*

My feet drifted down the ice-crunchy steps someone was kind enough to salt at some point. I pinched the coat closed at my throat. "You always loved Christmas. No wonder you chose to pass away during Christmas in July." I swallowed the perpetual lump in my throat. "I've got to quit talking to you."

"Who?" A little voice startled me. When I jumped, so did the little girl. Giant marshmallows and bottles of sprinkles tumbled from the bag in her mitten-covered-hands.

"Oh, I'm so sorry!" I quickly knelt in the snow for the sprinkles and puffs of sugar.

"I'm sorry I scared you." She took the bottles and put them back in the bag, but when I collected the marshmallows, she giggled, her smile lacking two front teeth. "I can't eat those. Mommy doesn't believe in the five-second rule."

Snow soaked my tights and froze my skin. I pushed off the ground and dropped the marshmallows. She took in my wet knees but asked if I was crying. I swallowed and swiped my face with the back of my hand. Sure enough, my skin returned wet with tears I hadn't known I'd shed.

"I think I have a cold," I lied.

"You were talking to your mom," she didn't ask. Damn kids and their inability to hide their nosiness. "She died, didn't she?"

My eyes welled while I nodded, helpless in the face of her honesty.

"I know. That's sad. She used to let me smell her roses when she was cutting flowers."

My heart clenched at the idea of Mom being so ... maternal.

"Mom told me to pour salt on your steps so you didn't slip in the snow. I'm not good at it yet. Someone told me that if you put salt in front of a door, it traps ghosts inside your house. Were you talking to her ghost?"

"Brielle!" a woman cried. She pushed a stroller and shoved a box near what I assumed was a baby underneath a canopy. The wheels hummed across the gritty distance between us. "Please, I'm not sure what she's said to you, but she has no filter. I'm so sorry if she was rude."

The mom took her child's hand and made her hold the stroller. Brielle retracted the canopy over the baby inside.

"This is my baby brother. Last year I asked Santa for a sister for Christmas. Either Santa's not real or he has trouble reading."

Her mother's eyes bugged at her child before they filled with apology up at me again.

I couldn't help my sympathetic smile. "It's okay. Honesty is a virtue, right?"

She coughed a nervous laugh. "Maybe, but it doesn't spell a future filled with friendships."

"Truer words were never spoken." I could relate to this child.

Brielle piped up like she was ready to protest or ask me to explain what that meant, but her mother shushed her, then she took note of the spilled marshmallows. "Oh, Bri—"

"It's my fault," I confessed. "I startled her."

"She was talking to a ghost," Brielle said.

A man called, "I'm coming! Wait, I'm right behind you!"

The woman twisted with a sigh. "Go back in the pantry and get the other bag of marshmallows, please? Brielle had an accident."

Brielle attempted to argue, but her mother's expression silenced her. "Cover your brother back up, Brielle. We don't want him getting cold." The stroller shook with the baby's movements. His mother sighed and thanked her daughter for waking him up after she'd just gotten him to fall asleep. "No rest for the weary," she said my way like I could relate. Meh, I guess I could, though my baby was a seventy-seven-year-old woman before passing.

The man reappeared with a fresh bag of marshmallows. The woman looked back at me while she waited on him to close the distance.

"Your daughter said you had her salt my stairs so I wouldn't slip. Thank you," I offered to the pair.

They each gave *the* sympathetic smile.

The man said, "She was a nice lady. Brielle used to ask her a million questions while she was gardening. Your mom patiently answered every question." *Add that to the list of things Mom never did until settling here.*

"Gave me a chance to sleep during my pregnancy." His wife smiled; gratitude replaced the prior sympathy. "She got to meet Bryce before she passed, and she just adored him."

Inadequacy assaulted my ovaries. I never made Mom a grandmother. Then again, I never thought she wanted anymore babies in her world.

Brielle and Bryce.

Brogan.

There were a lot of Br names in my world.

"She was definitely patient," I lied with a smile down at the little girl she'd indulged. Mom was anything but patient when *I* was Brielle's age, asking a billion questions, wanting to know *why, why, why* about everything. *Did she look at this little girl like a second chance to do better even though they weren't related?*

I nodded, tried to keep my expression from belying how ridiculous I thought their cutesy little cliche family names were. "I'm Kamryn, but friends call me Kamrie."

"Oh, like the car?" Brielle blurted. I grinned and almost asked if she and Brogan were related. Instead, I praised her observational skills. "You, my new friend, have the makings of a future reporter. Kids don't notice those things anymore."

Her mother shrugged. "I don't let her have a tablet or phone."

Brielle's lower lip popped, and she kicked one of the fallen marshmallows. "All my friends have them."

"I bet none of them are as smart as you," I said, knelt with my hands on my freezing knees. "You're going to be an investigator while they're all lost in video games."

"I'm going to be an actor like Uncle Brogan." She smiled again. The clouds of my breath ceased once more.

"You're related to Brogan?"

Her mother nodded. "I'm his sister, Brandy. This is my husband, Brandon. Since you know his real name, I'm assuming you're a friend of Brogan and not Tom Snow? Did you go to school with us? I'm sorry I don't recognize you."

I waved a hand. "No. I met Brogan at a writer's conference in June. He was being interviewed."

Her lips tilted into a wry grin. "But you learned his real name? Must've gotten intimately acquainted."

Brielle got her blunt lack of filter from her mother.

I chewed my lip and looked at the snow.

Brandy added, "You should take it as a compliment. He doesn't give his real name to anyone. Even his family has to call him Tom when we visit. He only goes by Brogan when he's here visiting, which, as of the last few years, is only for Christmas and Easter. This year it wasn't even for Easter. However, he did come for a sudden visit in July. Seemed like he had something on his mind and needed to cry on his family's shoulder."

I wasn't sure what to say or what to make of that. Was it good? Bad? Did she approve or disapprove?

Brogan lived here! This was home! Well, when he was home.

Her husband Brandon interrupted the awkward silence. "Are you moving into your mom's house or putting it up for sale?"

"I haven't decided. Not much an investigative journalist can write about in this town. It's too ... perfect."

They nodded. Brandy said, "So, write about other places and live here. It is a wonderful place. We had a blessed childhood. Great area to raise a family. You know, in case you ever wanted one."

Thank goodness for the darkness. My cheeks were sure to be bright pink.

Brandon said, "If you decide to sell, let us know if you'd like me to clear the gutters and repaint the shutters so you get top dollar."

"Oh, that's so kind of you. Were you the ones who kept my yard and put up these lights?"

Brielle nodded voraciously with a proud smile on her toothless face. "That was my idea. The lights. You like them?"

"I do. Very much. You're great neighbors and you cheer my sad heart. Thank you."

"You're welcome. Can I help you garden if you stay? Will you let me pick roses?"

A warmth thawed my cold ache.

"Absolutely. Maybe you can show me what you learned from my mom. I don't know how to garden."

"What?" Brandy leaned back like she needed a better view. "Girl, we've got to change that! We're off to the cookie decorating contest. Would you like to join us?"

"Oh, I can't. I'm headed to Las Vegas in the morning, but thank you."

Brandy's smile expanded. "My brother lives in Vegas. If you see him, say hello and tell him to come home for Christmas. He might do it for you. Oh, and if you don't have anyone to celebrate with, we'd be honored to have you join us."

"Thank you. For all of it."

Did Brogan tell them about me?

"See you later, Miss Kamryn." Brielle waved over her shoulder. To her mom she said, "Uncle Brogan should marry her. I think Uncle Brylan needs to come pray for her because I might've trapped her Mom's ghost in there with the salt."

I cupped a laugh and turned away when they peeked over their shoulders like they feared I'd heard her.

When they were out of earshot, I said, "I see why you shared your wisdom with that one. Just wished you would've shared more with me. Leave it to you to make me jealous of a freaking seven-year-old."

I cautiously walked back up the crunchy steps and grabbed the large garbage bag. They'd placed Mom's trash can on the side of the driveway. I flipped the lid and hefted the weight into the bin. The first step in letting go of what was. Between waving at crowds walking into town for the festivities, I packed more bags, trekked out to the trash, and turned down offers to quit working to have some fun in town. They had no way of knowing this was the best thing I'd done for myself in months. For the first time in too long I had hope in the darkness and now I had a reason to return to the house I'd never wanted to step foot into again.

Though I sniffed every item, I packed Mom's clothes for donation. Instead of driving them to the church, I stacked them along the foyer. I could only handle so much letting go at a time.

Before I returned to my own luggage, I scribbled a name and address on an overnight shipping envelope, stuffed it in between my clothing, then zipped the suitcase on the last of my effects.

If I lived through the last leg of this journey, I'd buy a tree, donate her clothing, then step inside that church every Sunday after because I survived to do so.

However, if Elliot Meyers killed me, I'd get the evidence put in that envelope and sent to the feds if it was the last thing I did to take him down with me.

thirteen

BROGAN

GRAYER CHRISTMAS SPECIAL COMING SOON!

Don't miss the next volume in the Detective Grayer series! Just in time for Christmas! Pre-order now!

I walked past the promotional posters lining billboards, hotel marquees, even nostalgic lobby cards. At first, seeing my face everywhere was cool. Now, it was a curse. Especially still dressed in character as Grayer. I finished filming and sought refuge anywhere but my trailer. Jordan hovered like a wasp ready to sting me for the smallest misstep. Best I could figure, he'd gotten himself in trouble with bookies and the more desperate he became to keep his life, the harder he made mine like I was an ATM.

"Hey! Hey!" The devil chased after my latest attempt at personal space. "Don't forget, you have an in-person interview to promo the newest book and the Grayer Christmas special."

"That interview isn't until tonight," I barked without looking at him. "I need a shower."

He speed-walked to keep up beside me. "No, don't shower. You're already in full hair and makeup. Leave it. You can go live on social media, surprise the audience, jog their excitement then appear as Detective Grayer in honor of the special."

"I just sweat my balls off in a trench coat under hot lights and a heated set because everyone else was cold. I'd like to take a shower. Damn, Jordan. What happened to you? When we started, you were amazing. I did my part, wrote the books, appeared on set every time I was scheduled to film. You booked my events and made deals, you know, stayed in your lane. Now, you're like a drunk driver swerving into every lane that isn't yours, no care for who you hurt. Back off."

"But the fans love Grayer. It's not about you or me. It's about them and what's best for the promo."

I stopped short and inspected his forehead, the sunshine glaring off his polished dome. Something was seriously wrong. I knew it with everything inside.

"I need sunglasses to look at you. The glare is hurting my eyes."

"That's not nice."

Of course he could dish it but not take anything close to his own cruelty. Damn narcissist. Didn't care about a single word I'd just said.

"It's the sweat added to your spit shine, there." I pointed. He swiped his forehead and cast a nervous look around us. "You afraid the mob's gonna disappear you in the desert if *I* don't make enough money on this one? Don't you have other clients to take your mistakes out on?"

I didn't give him a chance to respond. I left him there and hoped his thoughts haunted him. If the bookies didn't beat him to a pulp, I might accidentally do it for them.

When I unlocked my hotel suite, I disrobed and fished my phone from Detective Grayer's trench coat. I checked for any further texts from Kamryn after she'd broken the stalemate between us, but I'd yet to hear any further details or receive the email she said was coming in case the worst happened. I stared at her last two texts.

The shark just bit my line

I'm reeling

What did she mean by *I'm reeling?*

Context clues spelled a fishing metaphor, but what if she meant she was angry about something? Would that be in the email? Did something prevent her from sending it? I wanted to call, but if she was in a place where my call would jeopardize her cover, I couldn't handle causing her harm. Twiddling my thumbs wasn't an option. I put them to work instead.

Hey Special K

Been thinking of you all day 🖤

Director said my performance was better than it was in months

Of course, Jordan is still a

Can't win

Finally got a break from filming

Have to do a stupid interview tonight

Wish I was having dinner with you instead

I'd take rice crispy treats and the hostage situation right now pretty please

When did you plan to send the email?

Confirm you're okay, please

I hated that she hadn't texted back during my shower. Hated even more what I was about to do, that I might lose her over it. When she was silent for months, I figured she'd deleted my number and our history in her brain. After all, it was one night. Jordan repeatedly spelled out as much. So did I, when over and over she popped into my thoughts. But, not only did she reach out when she was afraid of who she investigated, she didn't blame me for what Jordan said. An a-typical woman.

I buttoned my shirt, spritzed cologne, combed my hair, and considered calling my mother for advice on what to do when you planned to ruin the life of someone you loved in order to save it. After all, they were the ones demanding sacrifice. In my head, I saw a beating heart laid on a stone, a knife hovering just above.

Here goes nothing.

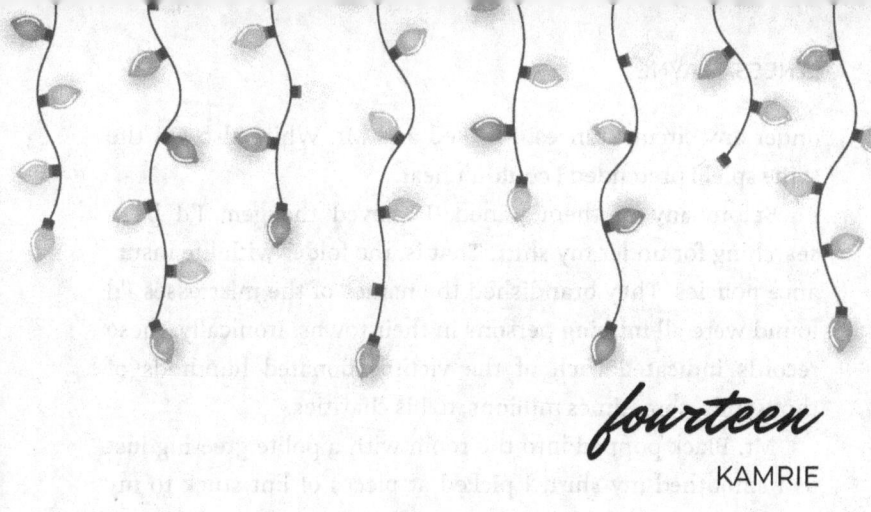

THE PENTHOUSE WAS everything I expected. Over the top. A showpiece of Elliot's power that younger girls and women wanted to fall into for the clout or a good showering of his money. If I were as young as I looked, my alias, Cassandra, fit the bill for the type he wined and dined. When it came to taxes, I wasn't playing, and he seemed tired of my no-nonsense attitude after several hours of my foray through his financial records.

"I'm going down to the craps table," he grumbled, all charm and flirtation from the private plane ride and tour of his humble abode gone. "Mr. Black is here should you require anything. He knows how to contact me if you run into any snags."

"Yes, sir," I said. "Good luck."

"I'd have better luck if you were to blow on my dice."

My chin jerked up from the file I perused.

"Last chance to join me ..." he trailed like he hadn't just gravely offended me.

"I'll pass, thanks."

"Suit yourself." He ducked out of the doorway. I heard him telling Mr. Black to keep an eye on me, not to leave me alone under any circumstances. Mr. Red and Mr. White also got the same spiel I pretended I couldn't hear.

Before any of them joined, I shoved the gem I'd been searching for under my shirt. That is, the folder with life insurance policies. They brandished the names of the mistresses I'd found were all missing persons in their towns. Ironically, these records indicated each of the victims donated hundreds of thousands, sometimes millions, to his charities.

Mr. Black popped into the room with a polite greeting just as I smoothed my shirt. I picked at pieces of lint stuck to my hoodie. For another hour I wrote notes on my pad, used a calculator, pinned my pencil between my teeth when flipping through pages of astronomical figures, receipts. I asked for Mr. Red and Mr. White to hand me folders and replace others into their rightful cabinets. When I gleaned they were sufficiently bored into trusting me, I leaned back in my chair and stretched, noted more lint on my hoodie, picked at more.

"I love my job, but I suck at wearing black when working with physical paper. I thought Mr. Meyers would've moved with the times and scanned his documents into his computer."

That earned a commiserating nod from Mr. Black. "Sometimes he's too analog for his own good."

Was he onto me? Allowing me to do this anyway?

Maybe I was overthinking?

I stood, grateful when nothing crinkled or gave me away. I'd purposely worn leggings that pilled like mad. They grabbed the tiniest of offending particles. I also scattered tiny scraps of paper on my chair for a moment such as this. I swiped my bottom, tried looking at myself over my shoulder. "Mr. Black, will you please tell me if I have junk on my pants?"

Mr. Red cleared his throat and watched me swipe my bottom and legs several times. I bent over to brush the length of my leggings, caught Mr. White's suspicious stare in my periphery.

"You missed, well, up, closer, yeah, right there," Mr. Black instructed. Before long he and Mr. Red laughed at my helpless shrug. I pulled the hoodie over my bottom, but it was too short and rose above my linty butt. To my shock, Mr. Black reached out to help end my charade, but quickly yanked his hand back when he realized he was almost inappropriate.

"I have a solution," Mr. White volunteered, a mite polite, though annoyed. "The hotel has shops downstairs. You could buy new pants."

Mr. Red nodded. "Mr. Meyers would happily buy you something to wear if you're uncomfortable."

"Well, gentlemen, the problem is, Mr. Meyers specifically told me to change into something comfortable, and these are my most comfortable leggings, but now I remember why I stopped wearing them in public. I may have to take him up on that if I venture downstairs to blow on his dice."

Mr. Black swallowed while I pretended not to know I'd said something awful.

Mr. White lifted a phone, told Mr. Meyers my predicament, hung up, then smiled politely at me. "Mr. Meyers instructed me to escort you downstairs. He's on a winning streak, but when he's done, he'd like to buy you new clothes."

"That sounds wonderful." I dusted my palms. "Lead the way."

fifteen

KAMRIE

THE GLITZY SHOPPES filled with tacky threads meant for partying or clubbing. Not comfort. Pretending to try things on was misery when keeping the stolen folder from falling apart. I tossed clothing over my hidden treasure, prayed they wouldn't inspect as they asked to see each item, snap a pic, send them to Elliot Meyers because the spoiled brat was too busy to buy me something in person. He wanted me pretty when I blew on his dice—his direct quote to Mr. White who watched me like a Loomis agent guarding a case of money.

I felt more like a prisoner than a freelance auditor and accountant. I said as much when I let my frustration show.

"That's it. I'm done. I hate everything in this store. I don't want to go shopping. I'd rather retire to my room and take a nap. Too much information, stimulation, noise, and on top of it all, I have to pee. Gentlemen, I'd also like my privacy."

The men frowned and followed my empty-handed trek out of the boutique. Mr. Black said, "Mr. Meyers won't be pleased if you don't go to him in person and let him know you're clocking out for the day."

"Oh? So is *this* pretty enough to wear onto the casino floor?" I gestured to my appearance.

Mr. White shook his head. "It's unacceptable. I'll walk you to your room. You'll be staying in the penthouse guest room."

I shook my head. "That wasn't part of the agreement. I was told I'd have a room in the hotel."

"And that's exactly what the guest room is," Mr. White insisted.

"I don't want to go upstairs yet."

"We aren't authorized to leave you."

"I'm authorizing you." I turned toward the sign for the bathrooms.

Mr. Black stepped beside me. "I'm afraid it doesn't work that way once you're employed by Mr. Meyers."

"I'm a freelance accountant without an exclusive contract, therefore I am not one of his employees. I'm a free agent. Do you get bathroom privileges, Mr. Black, or do each of you watch each other take a piss to be sure you get your hours?"

None looked pleased that I didn't kowtow to minor intimidation.

"Do I need to call 911? Am I a hostage?"

Mr. Black flinched. "Not in the least. I apologize if we came off that way. He's very private and strict. We don't want to lose our jobs."

"Mr. Black. I need to pee. Please, step aside so I may use the restroom. If any of you joins me, I'm calling the police."

He stymied an accidental snicker like police couldn't help me.

I feigned frustration as I parted their presence for the crowded restroom.

"Excuse me, ladies." I wormed my way through a large bachelorette party primping in the mirrors and gossiping about celebrities. I locked myself behind a stall. Fight or flight lanced my veins and laid a pit of dread like a brick in my belly. My fingers trembled as I sat on the toilet and pulled the folder and the addressed overnight envelope from under my shirt. Peeking through the cracks in the door, I shoved the manilla folder through the small slit and ripped the sticky strip to seal the evidence inside with the jump drive and note I'd written to my contact in the justice department.

The flush muffled the sounds of my battle with stuffing the puffy package back beneath my shirt. I pulled my hoodie over my belly. I spent an unhealthy amount of time washing my hands. In the mirror, I saw the last of the large group of ladies exiting directly onto the casino floor from an entirely different door. My shoes squeaked on the tile as I spun and dashed to join them. They were so drunk they accepted me and concealed my presence in their boisterous cheering for the bride who stole all the attention.

My blood went cold when I saw Elliot Meyers with a crowd cheering for his apparent success. His arm wrapped the waist of a young woman in a cocktail dress. He held dice to her and she laughed as she blew on them, then clapped and squealed when he won. Like he sensed eyes, he searched the room. I shrank and followed my herd toward the gleaming golden-framed doors toward freedom. Everything inside urged me to sprint away from here and hop an Uber idling beside the curb. Panicking would catch attention and by now the men were sure to know I'd slipped away. I didn't fit, but they were so flamboyant and numerous in number, no one appeared to notice me.

We cleared the exit without incident. I tugged my hood over my hair and kept my eyes down, focused on their flashy stilettos. When they stopped for a crosswalk with heavy traffic, I stared at a pair I really liked and was about to ask the woman where she'd bought them, when on the flier-littered sidewalk, Brogan's handsome smile grinned up at me.

I crouched for one, but before I could read it, a bridesmaid bumped me and asked, "Hey, who are you?"

I looked into her liquor-flushed face, longed for their type of simplicity.

"There was a guy in the casino who pushed too hard. Figured I'd blend with y'all to escape him."

She threw her arm around me and squeezed me beside her so tight her breast bulged. Ironically, Brogan popped into my head. Sometimes, you just need a hug. I put my arm around her waist and hugged her back, grateful for the kindness in this stranger.

I didn't want to do this anymore. I'd had my fill and never wanted to experience this fear of losing my life ever again. I just wanted to get this package to a post office and flee, maybe track Brogan to his set and demand he take me for that dinner date his agent stole from us, let him sweep me back off my feet for another massage.

He had husband hands, made my stomach flutter like no one ever had, and in this sweaty haste to save my life from a man who might take it, along with that poor girl's in the casino because I wouldn't sleep with him, I wanted the option to be someone's bride one day. Maybe a mom to a little girl like Brielle. Or even become Brielle's aunt.

Was this panic planning? Or, was this what life flashing before your eyes was actually like? A litany of past love mixing with what could've been?

She pointed at the flier in my fingers. "Can I see this?" she asked.

"Sure." I nodded and noted a set of bolts drilled into the ground near her shoes. *Holy shit! That's a mailbox!* "Here." I passed the flier and shimmied free of her affection, slipped the overnight envelope from beneath my shirt and shoved it into the federal box.

Silent praise shouted in my head. No one but the mail carrier could access that box without a welding torch.

I did it! The story officially had wings! I'd gotten what I came for! Currently had a heartbeat! Oh, Mom, if you could see me! Amid their cackling and celebration, I fought tears.

"Oh. M. G! You guys!" The bridesmaid with the flier shouted. The throng moved through the crosswalk and I shifted with them like we were one sequin-soaked creature. "This says that Detective Grayer is, at *this* moment, at the hotel next door!"

Brogan! Next door! Right now! So close! I had to get to him!

"Let's sneak in! Crash the party! Get his autograph!" Three of the ladies stacked ideas in rapid fire fashion.

If I wasn't so electrified with energy and hope, I'd have laughed at the idea they thought they could sneak anywhere when they were so sloshed they could barely speak without slurring.

"You could give him a lap dance before your wedding," one joked. They fell into a gaggle of giggles.

"Someone said he's from Evergreen."

"Duh!" Another said. "If you ever went to that old church in the historic district, you'd see his twin brother and think it was him."

The bride smiled back at her bridesmaids. "If she was any good at her duty, she'd know that's the church I picked to get married at just so he'd officiate. My pictures will look like I had a celebrity officiate my wedding."

Ugh. Poor Brogan. I remembered when people would invite Lori and me to parties on the hope that our famous mother would attend. After we caught on, we stuck to ourselves. Crazy to imagine Brogan as a preacher's kid *and* a preacher's brother.

Lot of pressure. Also crazy that I was living right next door to his sister for the better part of a year. Like fate. A Christmas miracle. Or divine providence.

I thought of my promise to attend church if I lived through this, echoed it inside my head. I was so close! If I could just figure a way out of here.

"What do you mean you lost her?!" Someone shouted from somewhere behind us. The bridesmaid who'd hugged me looked over her shoulder, then down at me. I nodded. She pulled me under her arm and had her girls close in tighter. "You didn't think to guard the other door?! I want her back now! Don't return until you have her. Dead or alive, dammit!" She gaped at me, eyes wide. The first sign of sobriety in the entire group.

"He's scary. And a dick. If you need a place to stay you can sleep in my room. I'm at the hotel across town." She shifted me so I was dead center of their group when we pushed through an enormous revolving door of the casino next door. Thank God I'd worn tennis shoes instead of high heels. Not only for being short among them, but in case I had to run for my life.

"Where is Grayer?" The bride leaned across the check-in counter. "We're staying here. How could I not see he was gonna be here?"

The bridesmaid beside me scrunched her nose and shook her head like a sly conspirator who wasn't in the least. I grinned.

The lady pointed and the throng turned like the bride was the lead goose in their flock. I told the girl I was staying here, thanked her for helping me get back to my hotel, that the man had no idea where I was.

"You call me if you need me, girl. We gotta stick together."

I promised and thanked her even if she neglected to give me her name or number. She was an angel I'd needed. I left their camouflage. My shoes squeaked on the shiny marble floor as I rushed to the convention hall in the opposite direction the clerk pointed them to. Smart. She'd protected the convention from invasion. If Elliot Meyers and his crew invaded, would she point them in the wrong direction, too? Somehow, I didn't think so.

sixteen

KAMRIE

I ROUNDED a corner like someone making a beeline with a bathroom emergency, saw a registration table. Lanyards littered the surface. I snagged one on my way past.

"Oh, excuse me, you can't enter without your—oh, never mind," she said when I pulled the lanyard with someone else's name over my hooded head. Brogan's muted voice echoed behind the closed double doors. A lady saw me and silently opened one and ushered me through, tapped her closed lips, pointed at the manned cameras perched on platforms. I nodded I'd be quiet and went inside what I expected to be a huge ballroom like the convention in Tahoe.

When I tucked into the nearest chair in only about two hundred, Brogan's answer paused mid-sentence. The ballroom was more like a glorified classroom. The stage was a tiny platform large enough to hold his and the interviewer's chair. *Shit!* That was a real anchor. As in, not retired like the one I'd watched interview him months ago.

She appeared annoyed by the disruption. "No more entrants, please? We're live." She looked at the camera in the center of the room and apologized to the TV audience.

Brogan watched me lower my hood. From here I saw his Adam's apple bob when he swallowed. My heart pounded so hard, the fabric should've shifted over my chest. Everything I'd felt in that hotel room rushed back without a hint of muting the deep attachment.

"Let's continue, shall we?" The anchor straightened her posture. "I'm sure we can all agree the excerpt you read was grittier writing than we've ever seen from you, but so is the storyline. In your previous novels, Grayer had a dark humor like a coping mechanism for his tough job. In the advanced copy I received, and devoured, by the way, I saw very little, if any, humor. Why is that?"

Brogan took a deep breath. Why did he seem nervous?

"Well, Trisha, it's simple. In this one, he's a broken man. He's divorced and bitter. The case he's on is enough to kill Christmas for anyone who reads the file."

My breath stuttered. That sounded an awful lot like the words I'd said to him during pillow talk.

"You have a beloved philanthropist kidnapping women who work for his very famous charity. He plays Santa every year. Grayer now sees every person on Santa's lap as a potential victim. Those he knows have been abused have been paid to stay silent. The ones who made reports were murdered. Every one of them received hush money from a fund the charity paid for with money they obtained through life insurance payouts from policies taken on previous victims. Very deep, dark plot."

I gasped and tears rushed to my eyes. Brogan's pained frown traveled the audience instead of my face. "What would you do if you found out every dollar you rounded up at the grocery store funded hush payments to victims that were then killed so those payments could be recouped or even doubled?"

The reporter took in the audience response, then her chin tilted when she saw me. I closed my eyes. Had she known my mother? When I opened my eyes, she attempted to return her attention to him, but lingered too long on my face.

"Forgive me, Tom. I know the audience would be horrified by that, which calls into question your publishing what reads almost like a horror novel at a time when family togetherness is what readers want."

"Trish, I disagree. There are many hurting people facing darkness during this time of year. Those who've lost someone they loved, for instance. I channeled that into Grayer because that's what Christmas is for him this year. I think it's okay to be honest about that. His wife left him because she got pregnant by another man. His father passed away after losing his battle with Alzheimer's. He's in the mood for justice."

What in the actual fuck was author Tom Snow doing?! Did he steal my story and my entire life to write a fucking book?!

'Tom Snow' added, "The perception of a Christmas miracle is in the eye of the beholder. We have our cliches and it's all merry and bright, but it's not for people in bad lives, living in fear, being exploited for gain of bad humans. You see a horror story. I see a miracle. He brings to light the dark deeds of a man exploiting Christmas and murdering people. I'd say that's pretty wonderful and should make everyone happy. He's saving lives, stopping the killer."

The audience, including me, clapped long and hard. Though tears of betrayal stung my eyes, I was grateful for his pointing out the hypocrisy of those who want justice, but only so long as it doesn't darken their pretty plans or the world they live in. The anchor included.

She lifted and lowered her hand until she had silence again.

"Excellent point. Grayer usually has multiple cases he's working in any given novel," she said, "but in this one, he's focused on only one case. Why?"

"Tunnel vision. Demand. Lack of supply. It's hard to find

good detectives willing to investigate true corruption, especially when many of them have been paid to look the other way or may even be in on the action. Grayer can't be bought and that makes him more of a hindrance than hero sometimes. He's bought answers from perps on the streets, but they can't bribe him in return. Incidentally, that's where his name comes from. He grays the lines, but he's not willing to let anyone else gray his. *He* is the grayer. He's also fiercely loyal to his partner."

She nodded and looked at me again, then her eyes darted up to the camera. The production team panned the camera over the clapping audience, then they gave her the spotlight once more.

"Were you inspired by anything else? A broken heart of your own?"

My brows dipped with Brogan's. "No, why?"

"Well," she smiled and dread filled my stomach. I knew *that* look because my mother played this role a few times in her career. "Your agent let it slip that you had inspiration for Grayer's heartache and the plot of this novel from an investigative journalist you had a fling with."

To my horror, the large screen on the wall behind them lit with the selfie Brogan had sent to me after we'd slept together. Next came the one with him kissing my cheek. A soundless close-up of only our faces came next, before the video of him kissing me filled the room with silent shock and awe.

"Isn't that Evelyn Krouse's daughter? She's the spitting image of her mother. You make a great pair."

Brogan's mouth opened and shut without answers while my hand covered my own.

"She's here, isn't she? In the audience. Supporting you in what you worked on together."

My eyes bugged and I shrank down like a student trying to sleep in class.

"No need for either of you to hide. Who else thinks they're adorable and we'd like to see Grayer happy for once?"

Nausea gripped my guts when, in my periphery, I caught Mr. Black inching along the back wall. Brogan's revulsion took a back seat when he noted the same.

Like he had in his interview in Tahoe, Brogan stood up. Instead of pacing the stage, he walked off altogether. The audience and interviewer gasped.

"Wait, Tom, I didn't mean to upset you. Please—" She silenced when he walked up to me and took my hand.

"My heart has been broken," he said before me, his voice still amplified by his personal mic. "Not because anyone cheated. Because *I* was cheated out of being in a relationship by my agent who stole my phone, read my texts, deleted texts, sent texts in my name. I've discovered he's burned many bridges in my life, kept me to himself under the impression that my acting contract includes an exclusive representation by him only. He's a fraud and he's taken too many good things from me."

I gaped, horrified.

"I'm praying he hasn't taken the best thing." Brogan stared down at me like he wanted to run with me.

I shook my head, my anger about the story on the back burner to my desire to sooth him. He tugged me gently to my feet. My palm inside his sweat so hard my flesh nearly slipped from his grip. He adjusted and intertwined his fingers in mine. I followed him onstage.

"Get her a chair, please?" The anchor rushed to give me hers. The crew shoved hers beside Brogan's then quickly gave her one of the simple folding chairs from the audience. "Mics. Please. Get her hooked up."

"That's not necessary," Brogan said and detached his to hold it before his mouth. He also refused to sit. "That man back there—" He pointed while I nearly pissed myself with fear. "—

is called Mr. Black. His *real* name is Darius Camp. He works for the true, real-life villain from Grayer's story, Mr. Elliot Meyers."

A collective gasp had not only my jaw on the floor. The anchor and the audience froze, stunned to silence. My fingers tightened in Brogan's hand.

"The justice department has the evidence to back everything I've written with the help of undercover journalist, Kamryn Kole, the daughter of the late, great Evelyn Krouse."

Mr. White and Mr. Red joined the room. Mr. White said something into his phone, hung up, then strode toward the stage with mafia authority. *Dear, God, please don't let us die!*

"She'd be so proud of the legacy she's left behind, because there isn't a braver journalist I've ever met. She risked her life to bring the truth to light in the face of caring for her ailing mother and then grieving her passing."

When the men mounted the small stage, Brogan tucked me under his arm and sent a soothing squeeze. "These gentlemen are the real-life detectives who advise me on the show and they're the inspiration for Detectives Hamill and, well, White." My body went numb and I sagged against Brogan's hold. "He didn't want to change his name."

Brogan kissed the top of my head. The anchor shifted from interviewer to reporter on the scene of breaking news. She signaled a camera man and held her earpiece like she listened, then said, "This is Trisha Shore coming to you live from Las Vegas where Author Tom Snow, known best for his role as Detective Grayer, has just confessed that his inspiration for the new novel and Christmas special is based on the real case of Elliot Meyers."

"Madam, if you'll cease your report until we finish," Mr. White, erm, Detective White, said. He shoved his blazer aside to reveal a badge hooked to his belt. Mr. Red and Mr. Black joined onstage. "Some months back we received a whistleblower tip that Elliot Meyers was responsible for the deaths of two interns for his charity. Darius Camp was brave enough to come forward and confirm there were at least twelve other victims we've recovered in the desert. In exchange for his cooperation, he is not being charged. He's a hero for helping us save future lives, including that of this young lady without whom we couldn't have sealed the arrest warrant for Elliot Meyers. Her diligence uncovered a money laundering scheme tied to a life insurance scandal. Mr. Meyers has been apprehended pending charges of murder, extortion, money laundering, insurance fraud ..."

As the list grew, I tucked my face into Brogan's chest and sobbed against his shirt. "Thank you." My voice cracked. "You did it."

"You did," he said near my ear. "I just used my fame, name, and connections for good." He kissed my temple, then straightened to his full height, urged me away from his chest so I had to face the audience once more. I swiped my fingers over my cheeks, came away with mascara-marred prints, but didn't care.

"Excuse me, Detective White," Brogan said, "if you wouldn't mind I'd like to make a statement."

The chattering audience hushed and waited.

"I'm officially retiring from television to surrender to the ministry." Brogan laughed at their shock and awe. "Just kidding. That's my brother. After this, you'll find me blackballed in the industry for my willingness to do the right thing. I gladly accept the fate. You might find me in B, C, maybe D-list movies, maybe as an extra in a sitcom, but Detective Grayer will be forcibly retiring at the end of the Christmas special. I will also be retiring from writing Grayer novels as the rights to Grayer are owned by a publisher and the series by a production company who cut ties with me when they found out I'd tricked them into filming a true story about their friend for the Christmas special that releases on Christmas Eve."

Brogan Slossel was a smooth sonuvabitch. The booing that ensued was such that social media erupted with millions of demands he be released of his contracts, calls for investigations into the production company, that they sell the rights to another company so Tom Snow could be free to act as Detective Grayer in the future. Because of this stir over his career, the subject of Elliot Meyers and the subsequent Christmas special kept the spotlight on Meyers and all involved to the point that demands for justice were met rather than the bad guys walking free.

And Brogan? Well, he won his lawsuit against his agent. Jordan was arrested for conspiracy to commit murder after he'd contacted Elliot Meyers about my true identity. He currently sits behind bars awaiting trial. His assets were dissolved to pay Brogan for damages.

By popular demand from readers all over the world, I traded my investigative journalist hat for that of Tom Snow's co-author. I have my own character in his show and within our novels. She's an investigative journalist, though.

Immediately after Brogan made waves in Vegas, we hopped a flight and relished how news still traveled slow in his home-town. They wouldn't find out until after New Years. We made it back to Evergreen Lake just before a blizzard grounded all flights. We found ourselves trapped in my house without power, forced to keep each other warm.

He'd helped me pack Mom's old things, let me keep what he insisted would be special one day, then we walked through the snow into the church for his brother's Christmas Eve service by candlelight. There, I activated my promise to attend every

Sunday. Though my name didn't start with a B, the little rebel introduced me to his family, then proposed without any of us expecting it.

Brielle has plans to be our flower girl *and* the ring bearer because she can do both jobs, her words.

"Welcome to the B Hive, honey." His mother embraced me first, then the rest of them followed suit.

After we'd trudged back through the dark town, soaked up to our thighs from climbing through the deep snow, Brogan warmed me up with his magic hands, among other things. He'd rolled onto his back beside where I still rested on my belly from the best massage ever. My ring glittered in the candlelight. I couldn't quit looking at it. He smiled and ran his fingers along my back.

"You forgive me for stealing your story?"

"I do. I'm grateful you can't mind your own business. That you didn't. I love that you see something wrong and do something. Action over words, but that you still back it up by using actual words in novels."

His fingers caressed my back. "We make a good team, Kamrie. I put out a poll to see if the audience wants me to bring you on as a co-author."

"You did what?" I leaned onto my forearms. "Brogan, if you want me to be your co-author, just ask."

He did. Just like his proposal, I obviously said yes.

"Best fucking birthday ever?" He kissed my temple.

"Best fucking birthday beyond a doubt."

I couldn't help sending a silent thanks to my mom for bringing us together in her own way. I'd have never found him without her, never been brave enough to push past my fears. Now, in the home she'd made for me before leaving me, I found myself adopted into a new family who all loved and valued my mother the way I did. Through them, she lived forever. Best Christmas ever.

****

Ready for the next book in the Evergreen Lake: Under the Mistletoe series? Check out Mistletoe Magic by Rebecca Barber.

evergreen lake

UNDER THE MISTLETOE

also by lynessa layne

about lynessa layne

Best known as the host of TropiCon Book Expo & Writing Convention, Lynessa is also a certified copy editor, freelance formatter, and *USA TODAY* bestseller.

She's a member of Mystery Writers of America and the Author's Guild with work featured in *Mystery and Suspense Magazine*. She was a finalist for Killer Nashville's 2022 Silver Falchion Awards for Best Suspense and Reader's Choice with volume 4 of her Don't Close Your Eyes Series, *Dangerous Games*.

In 2023, *Target Acquired*, volume 6 of her series, won the Silver Falchion Awards for Best Suspense and Best Book of the Year.

Lynessa Layne is from Plantersville, Texas. Married to a Lieutenant Commander, Lynessa has bounced around the south of the US until finally landing in the heart of sweet home Alabama.

She's an avid reader and music lover. As a child, she created music videos in her mind and played Barbies longer than most. In her teens she poured her angst into poems and short stories, but didn't start writing novels until 2014 upon falling in love with Charlaine Harris' long-running series featuring Sookie Stackhouse. Unable to find another series that followed the same characters through misadventures, she attempted to write what she wanted to read and came out with the Don't Close Your Eyes Series.

For a deeper look into Lynessa's past and what made her the writer she is today, check out her feature in the Knoxville Voyager Meet Lynessa Layne - Voyage Knoxville Magazine (knoxvillevoyager.com)

For more information on upcoming releases, swag and signing events, visit https://lynessalayne.com and sign up for her newsletter, Lit with Lynnie and join the Don't Close Your Eyes Reader Group or Lynessa's Layniacs Fan Club.

For information on TropiCon Book Expo & Writing Convention visit tropiconbookexpo.com

<u>Social Media</u>

https://www.goodreads.com/author/show/7992789.Lynessa_Layne

https://www.facebook.com/authorlynessalayne

https://www.instagram.com/lynessalayne/

https://twitter.com/LynessaLayne